BONE ADVENTURES

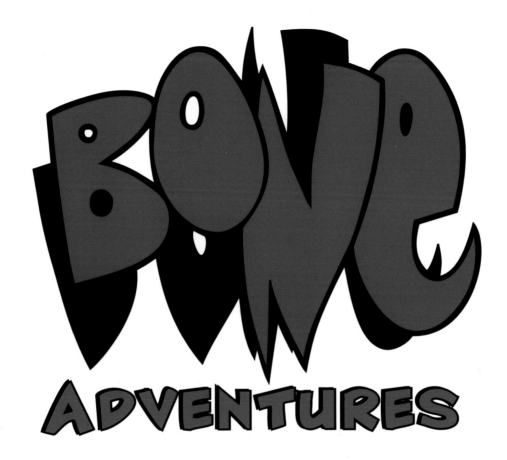

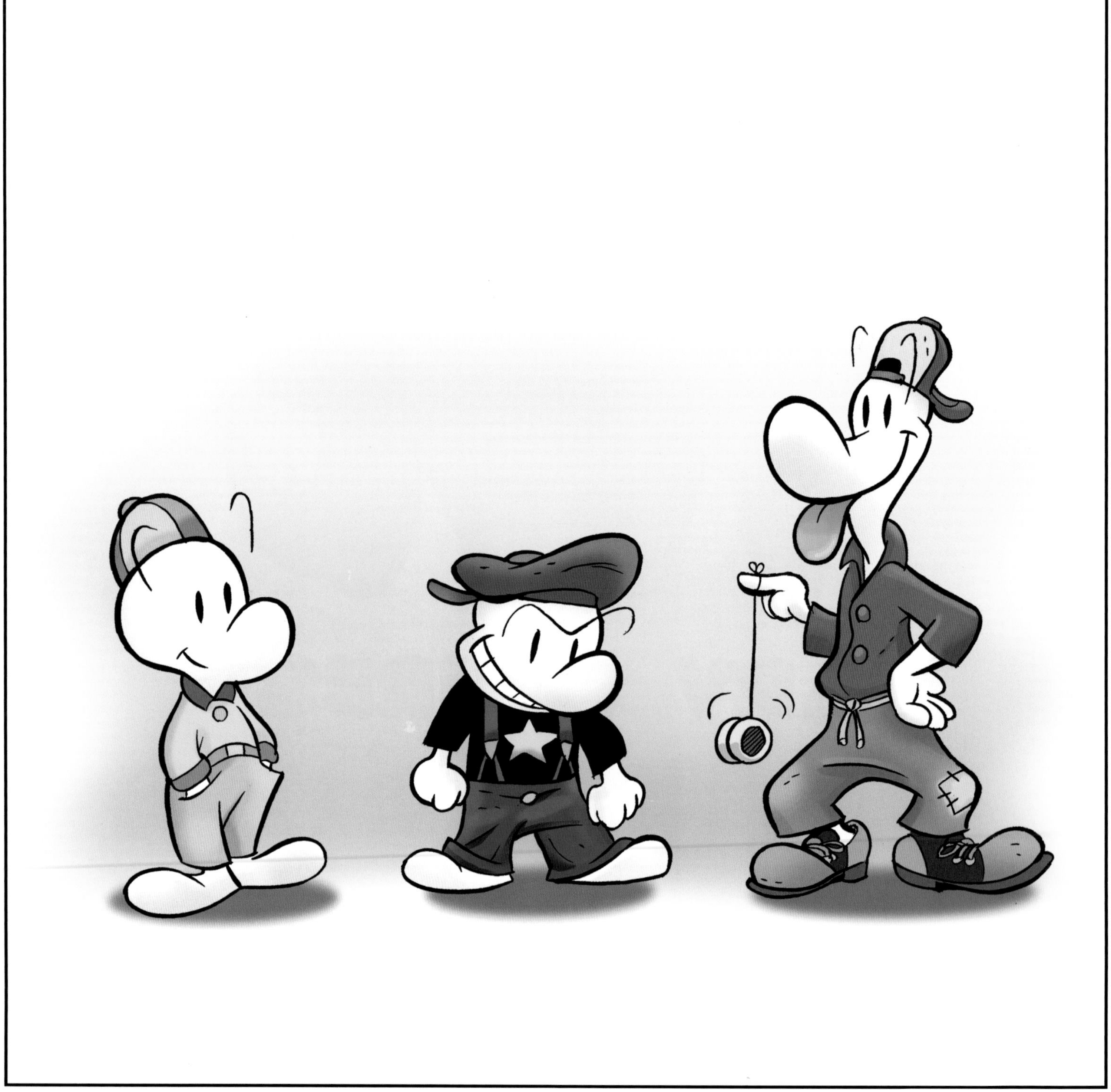

BONE ADVENTURES

BY JEFF SMITH
COLOR BY TOM GAADT

graphix

An Imprint of
SCHOLASTIC

Library of Congress Control Number available

ISBN 978-1-338-62068-9 (HC) / ISBN 978-1-338-62067-2 (PB)
10 9 8 7 6 5 4 3 2 1   20 21 22 23 24

Printed in China   38
First edition, May 2020
Book design by Jeff Smith and Charles Kreloff

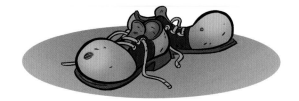

FOR VIJAYA

CONTENTS

FINDERS KEEPERS!

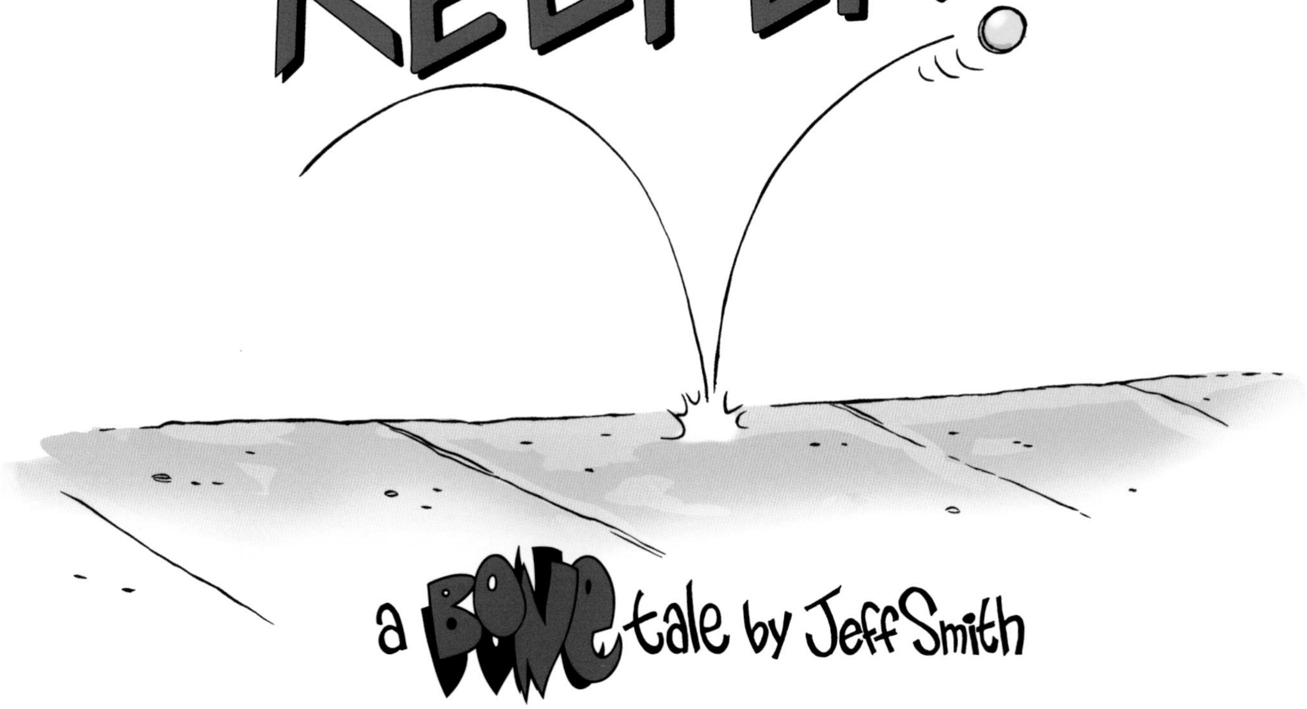

a BONE tale by Jeff Smith

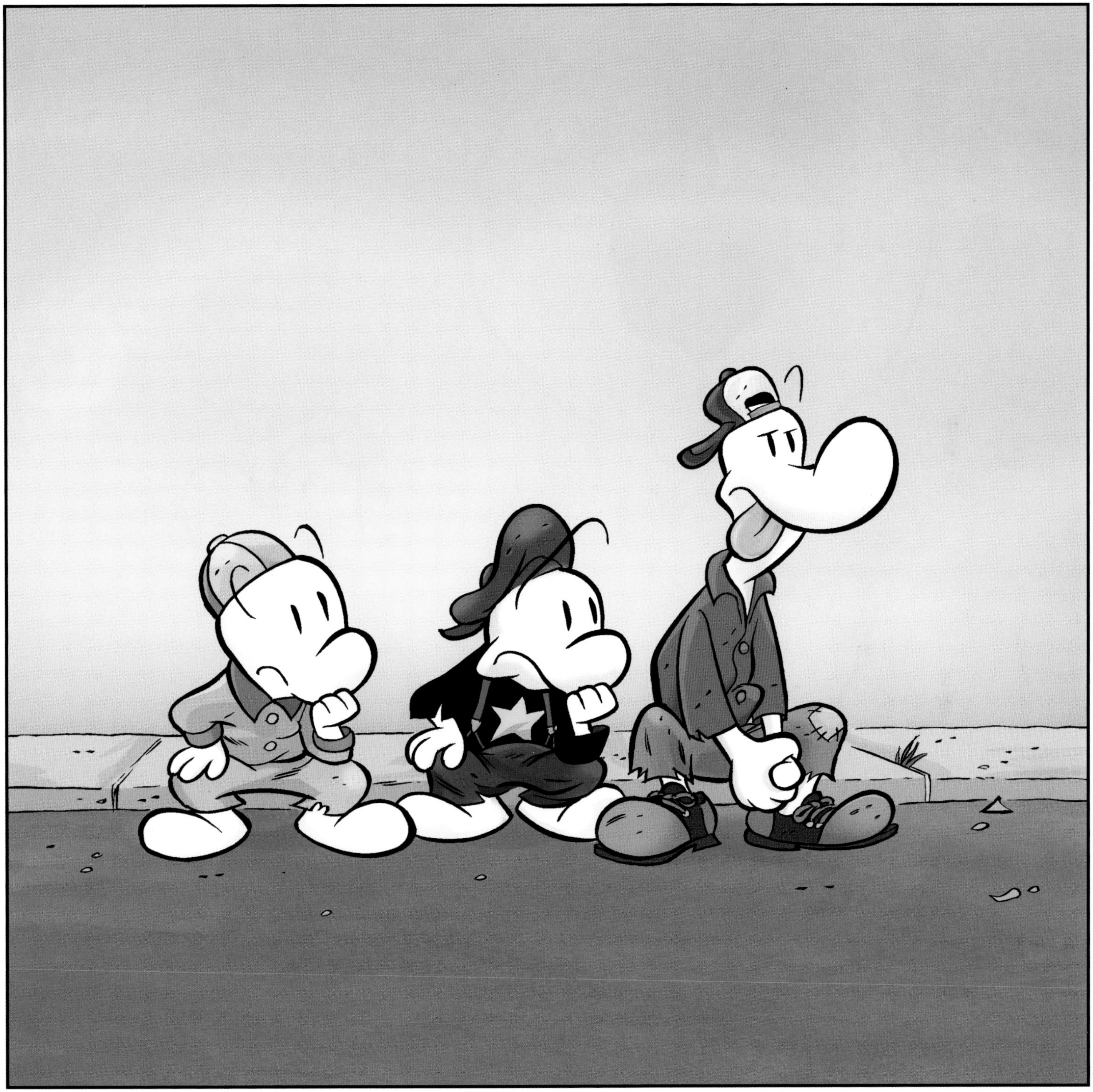

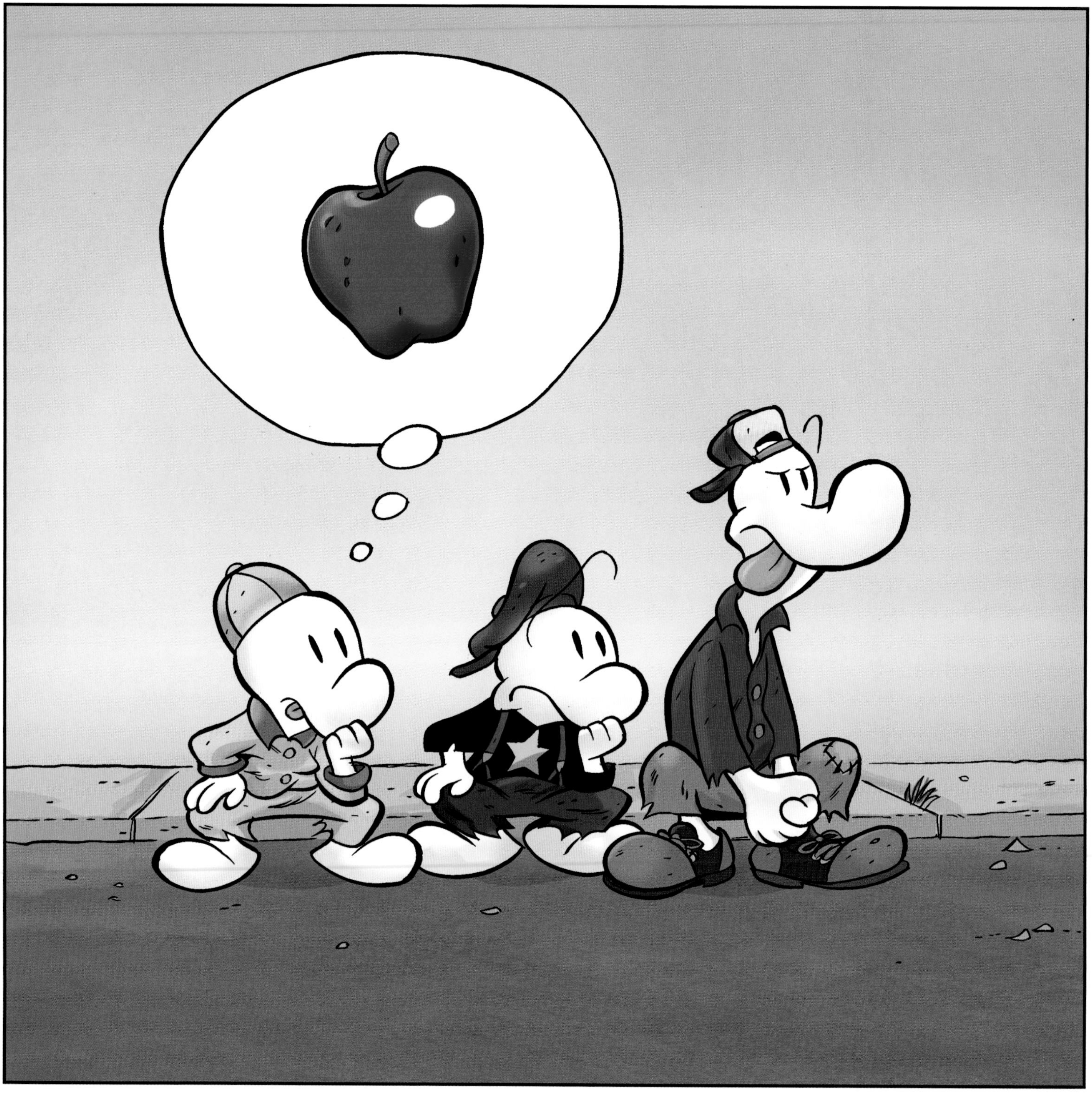

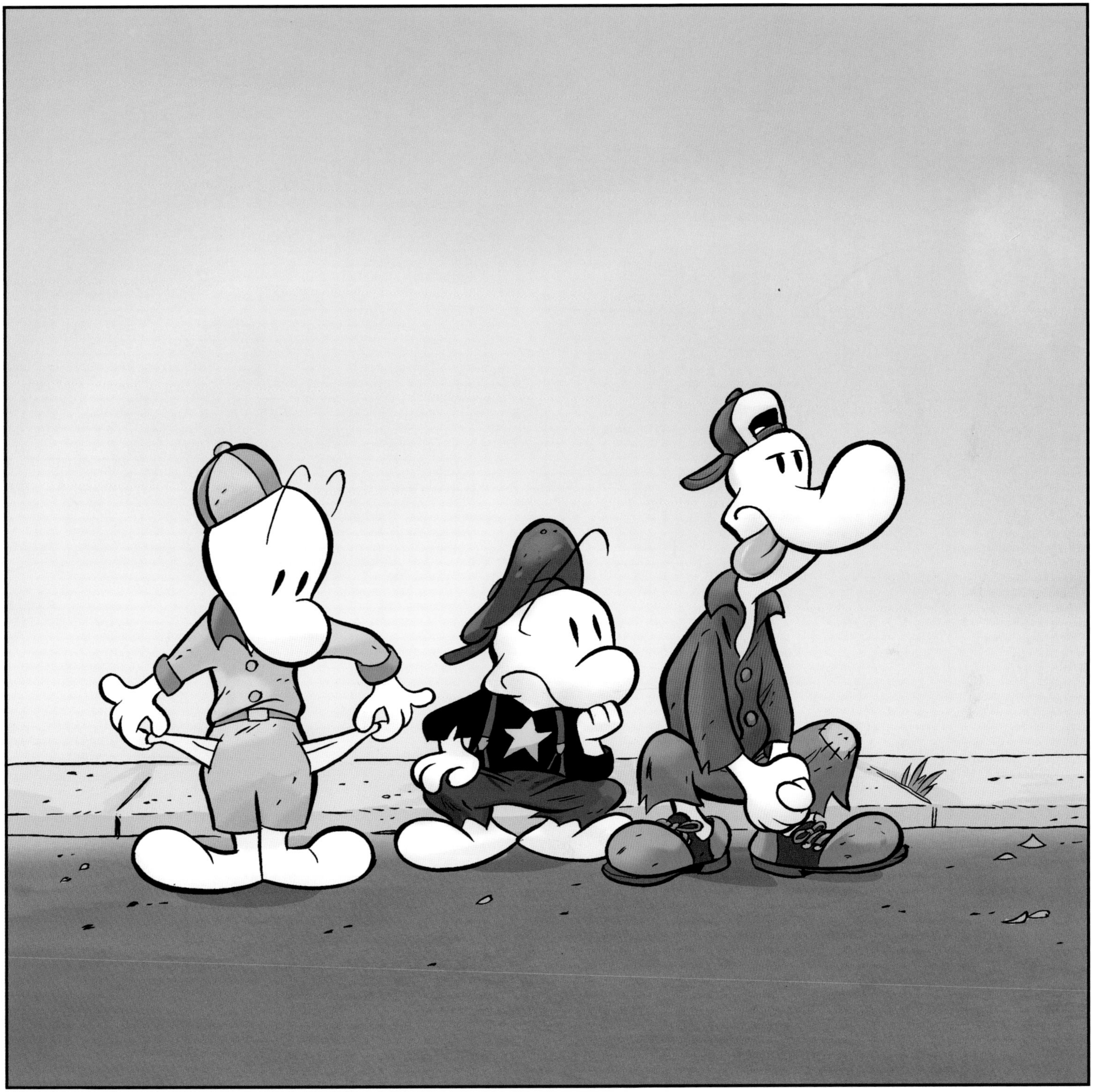

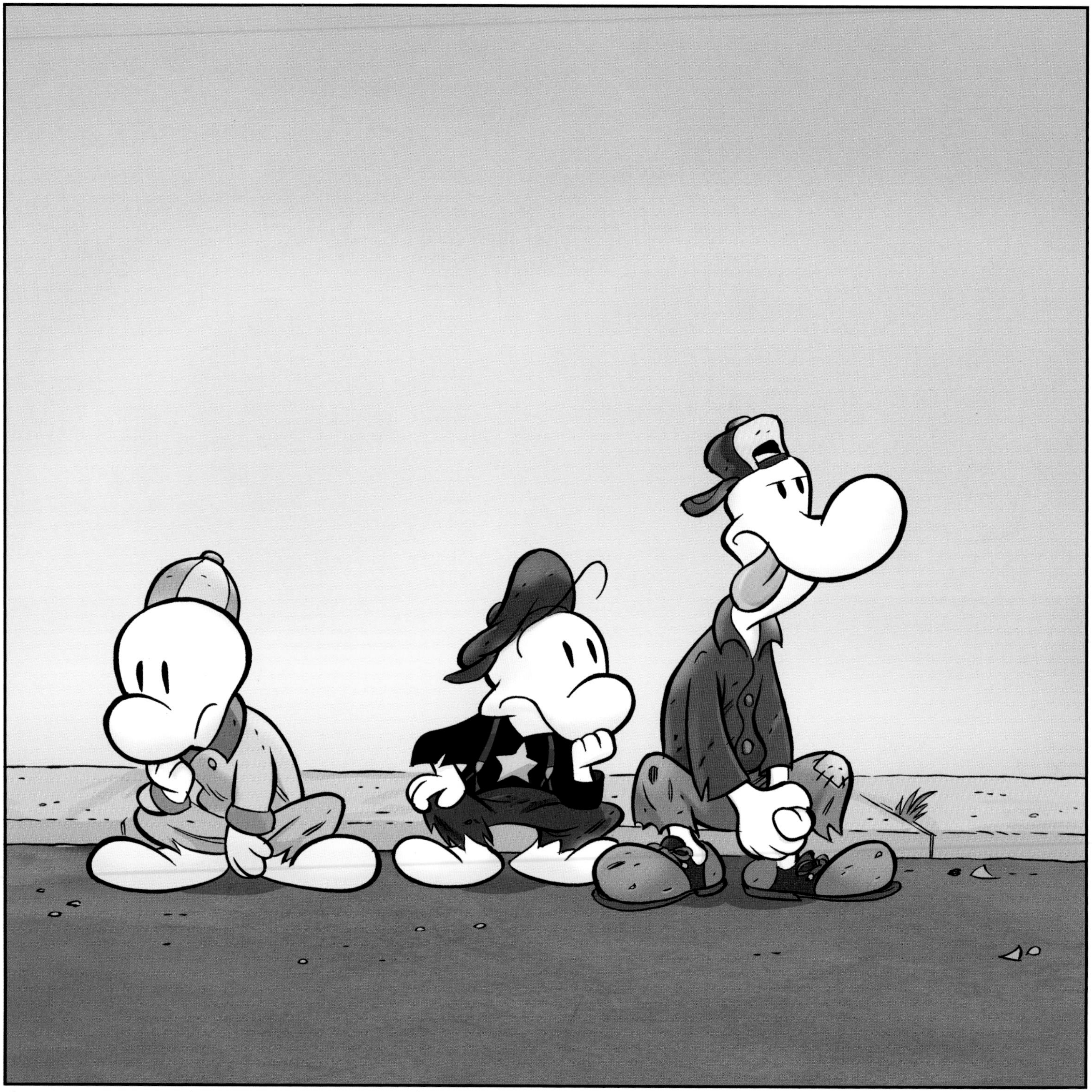

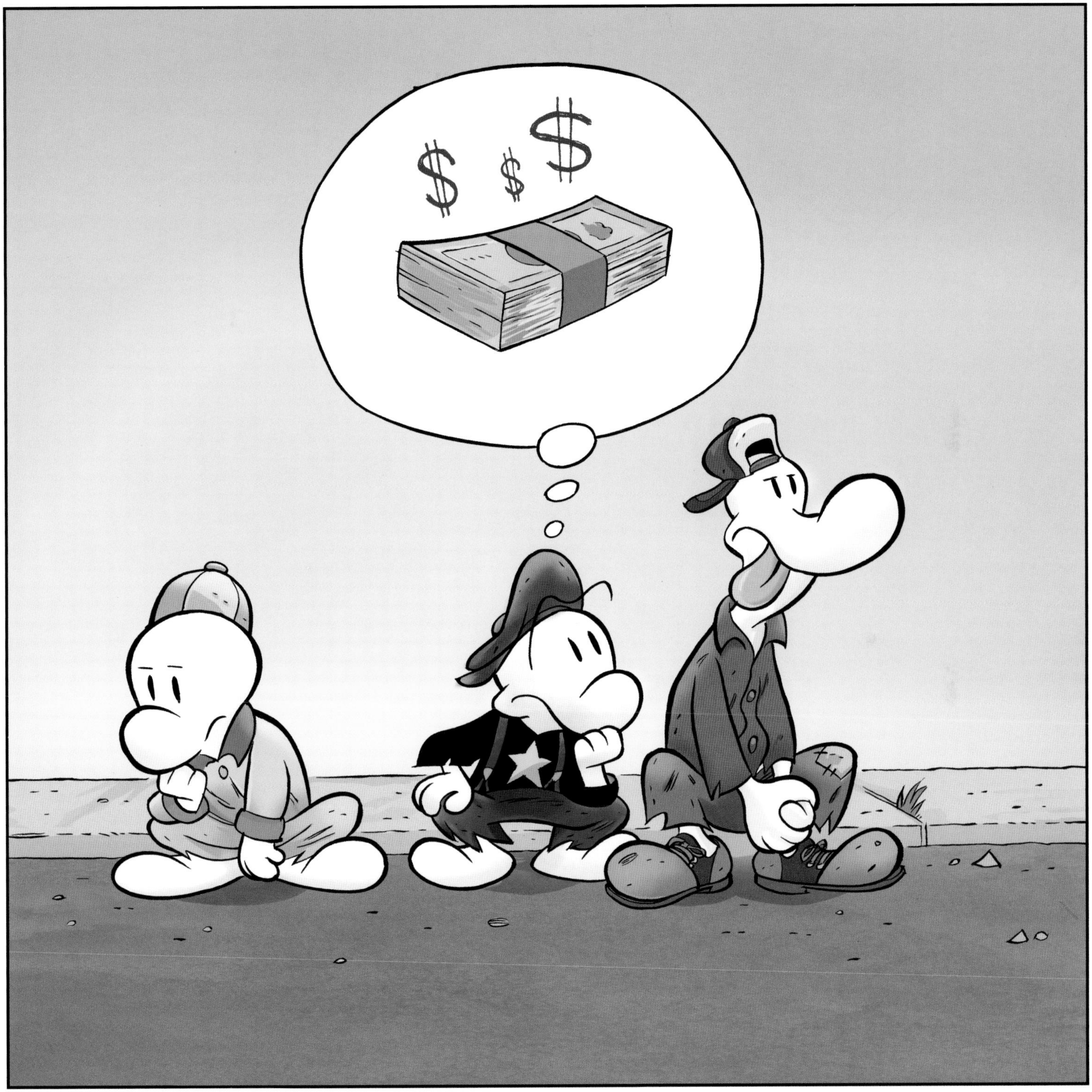

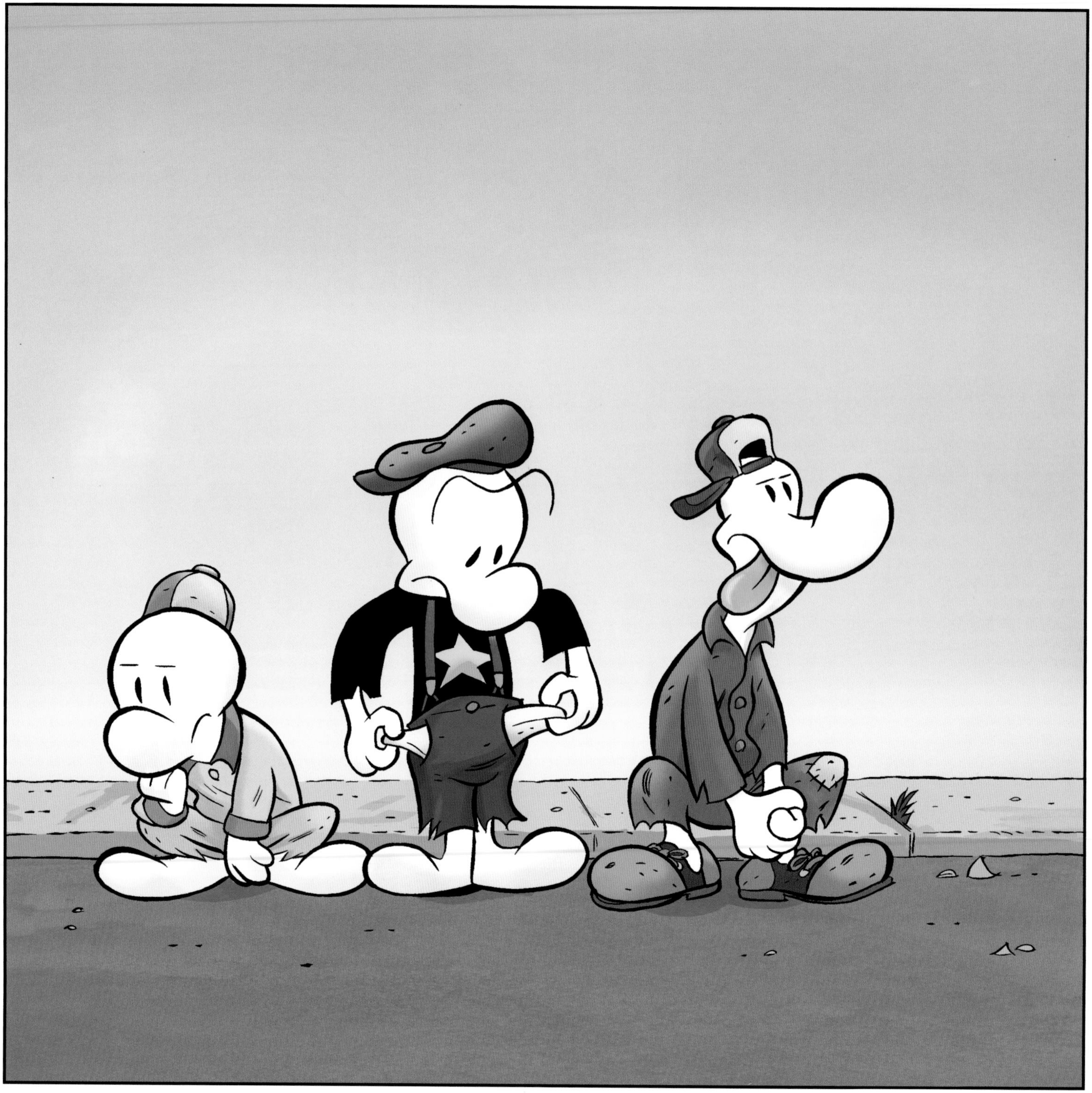

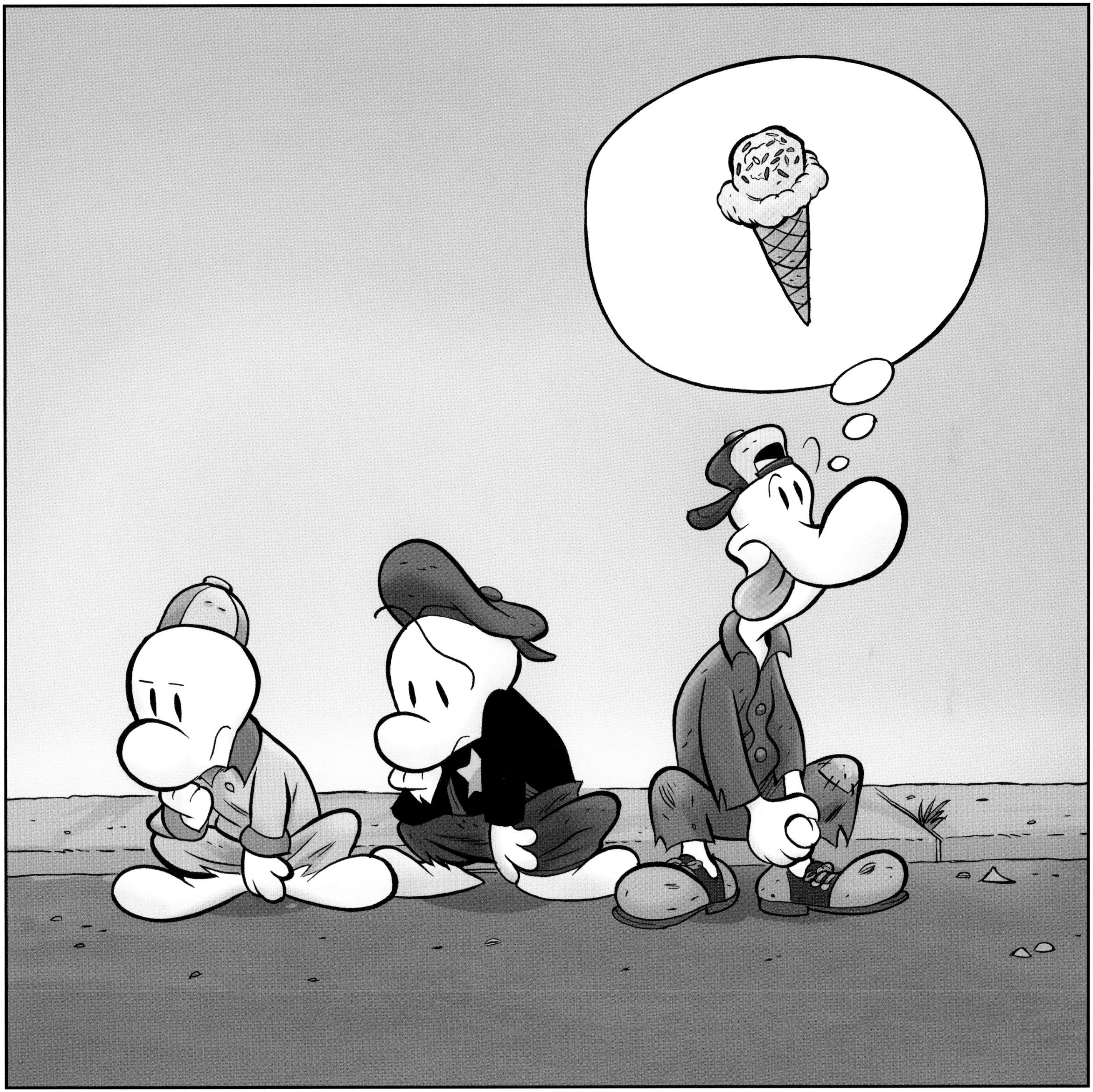

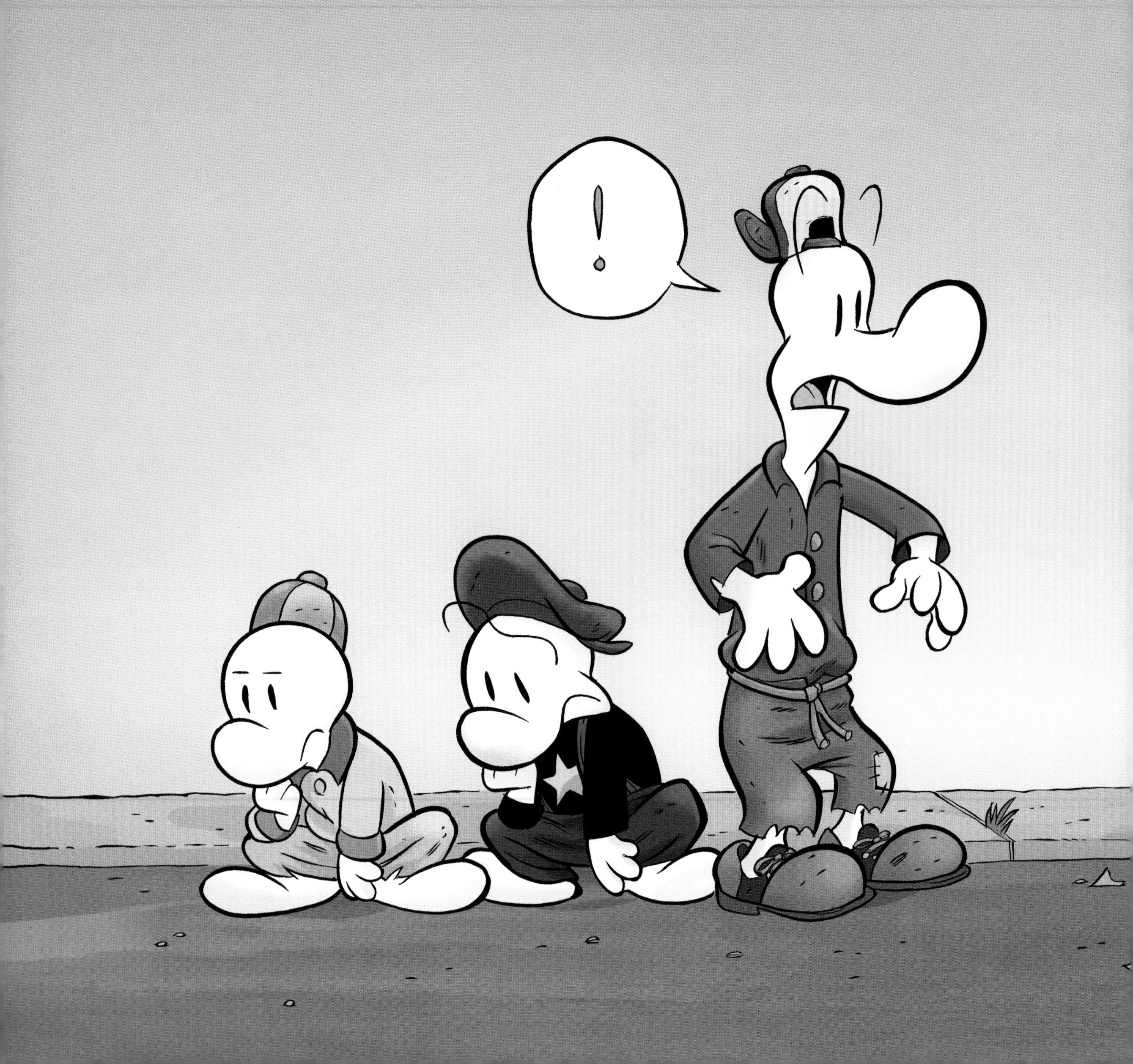
!

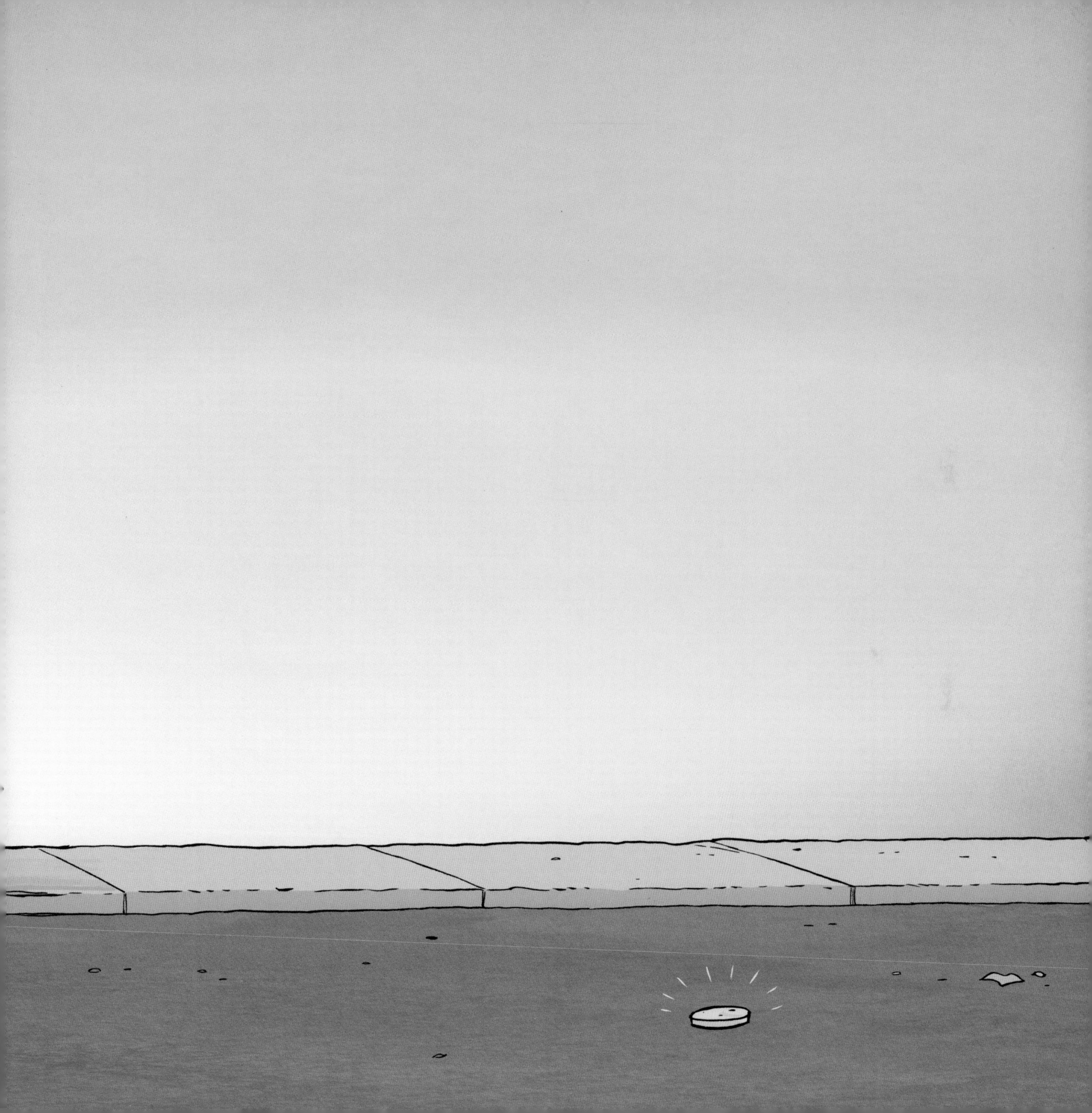

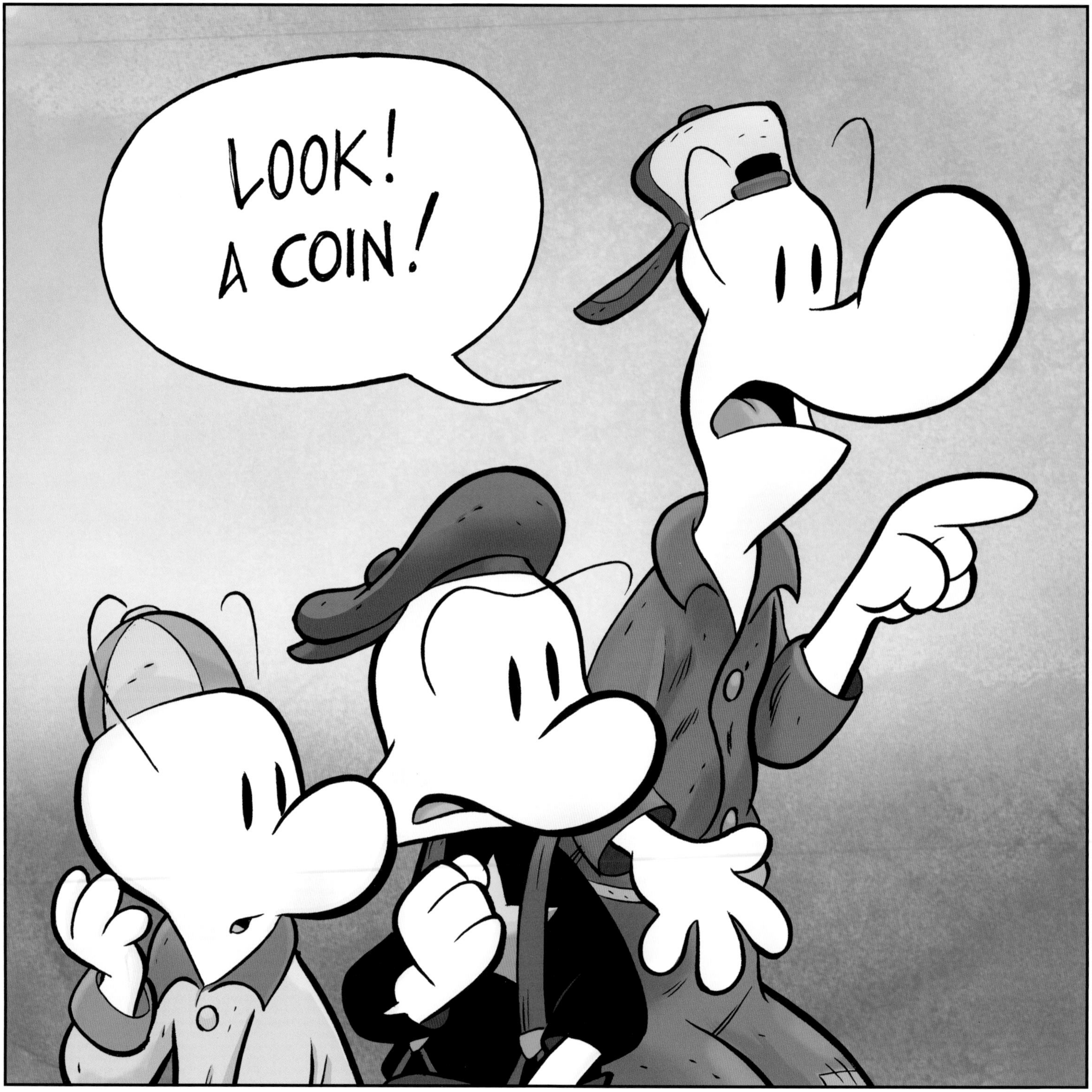
LOOK! A COIN!

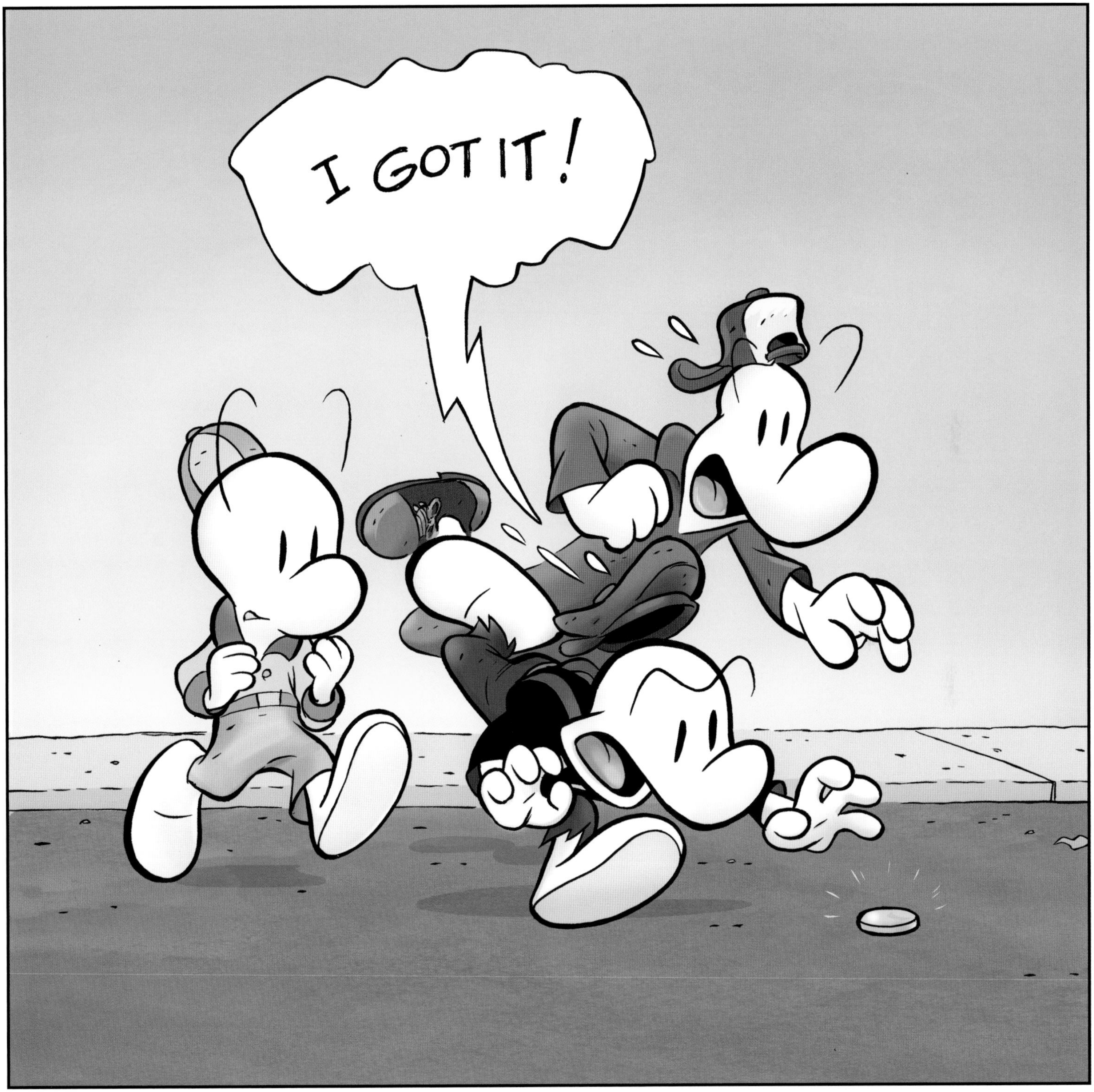
I GOT IT!

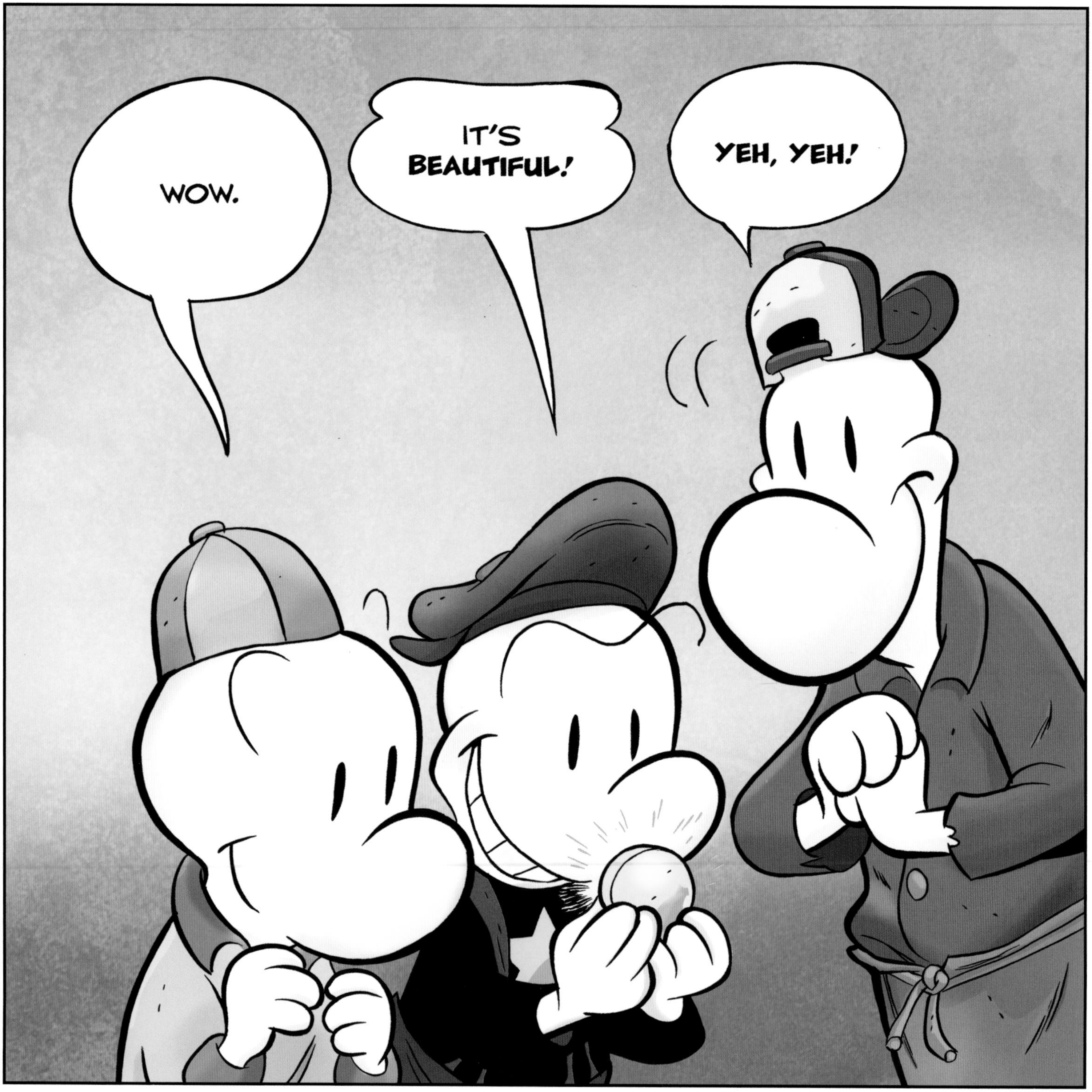
WOW.
IT'S BEAUTIFUL!
YEH, YEH!

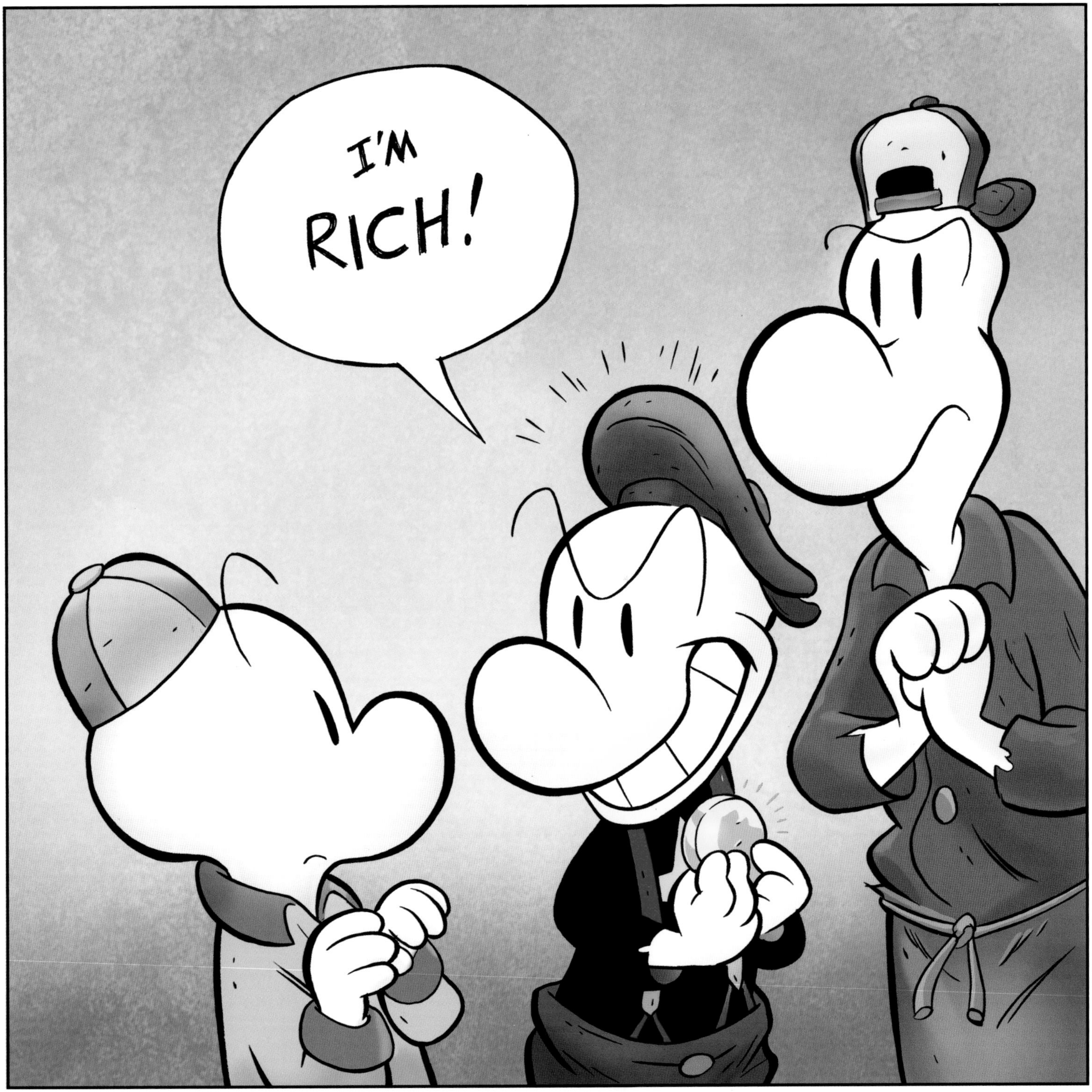
I'M RICH!

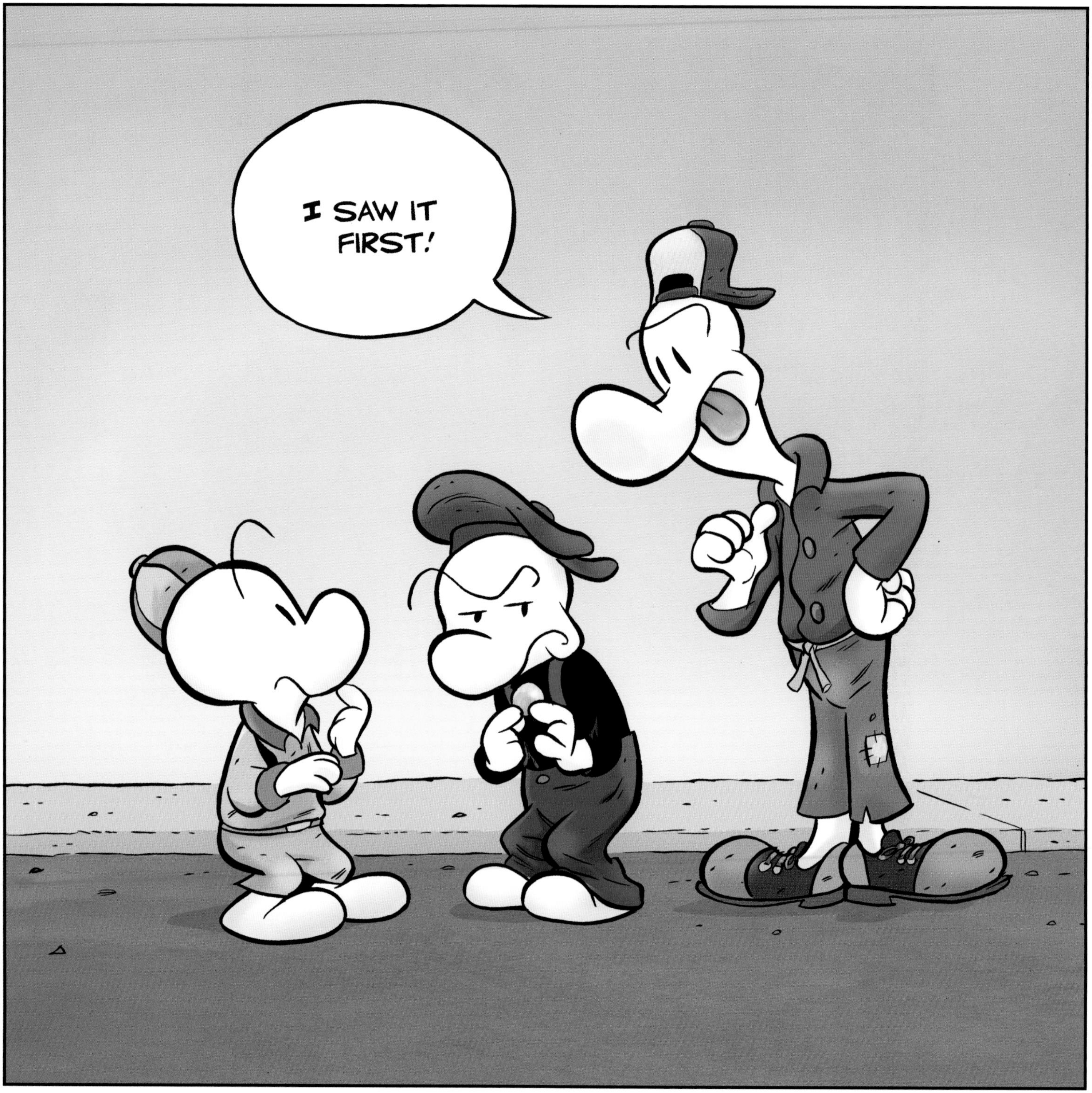
I SAW IT FIRST!

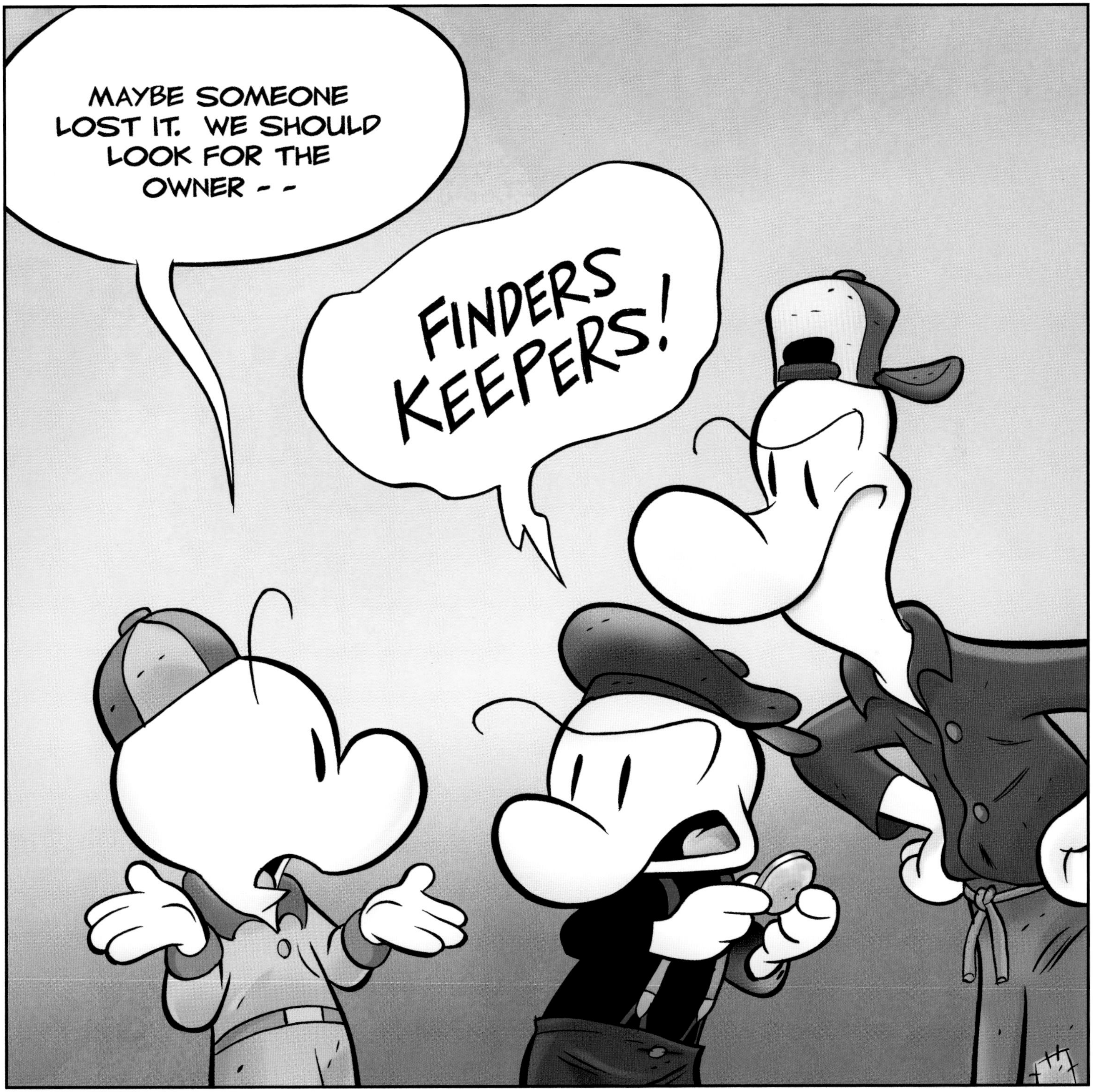
MAYBE SOMEONE LOST IT. WE SHOULD LOOK FOR THE OWNER - -
FINDERS KEEPERS!

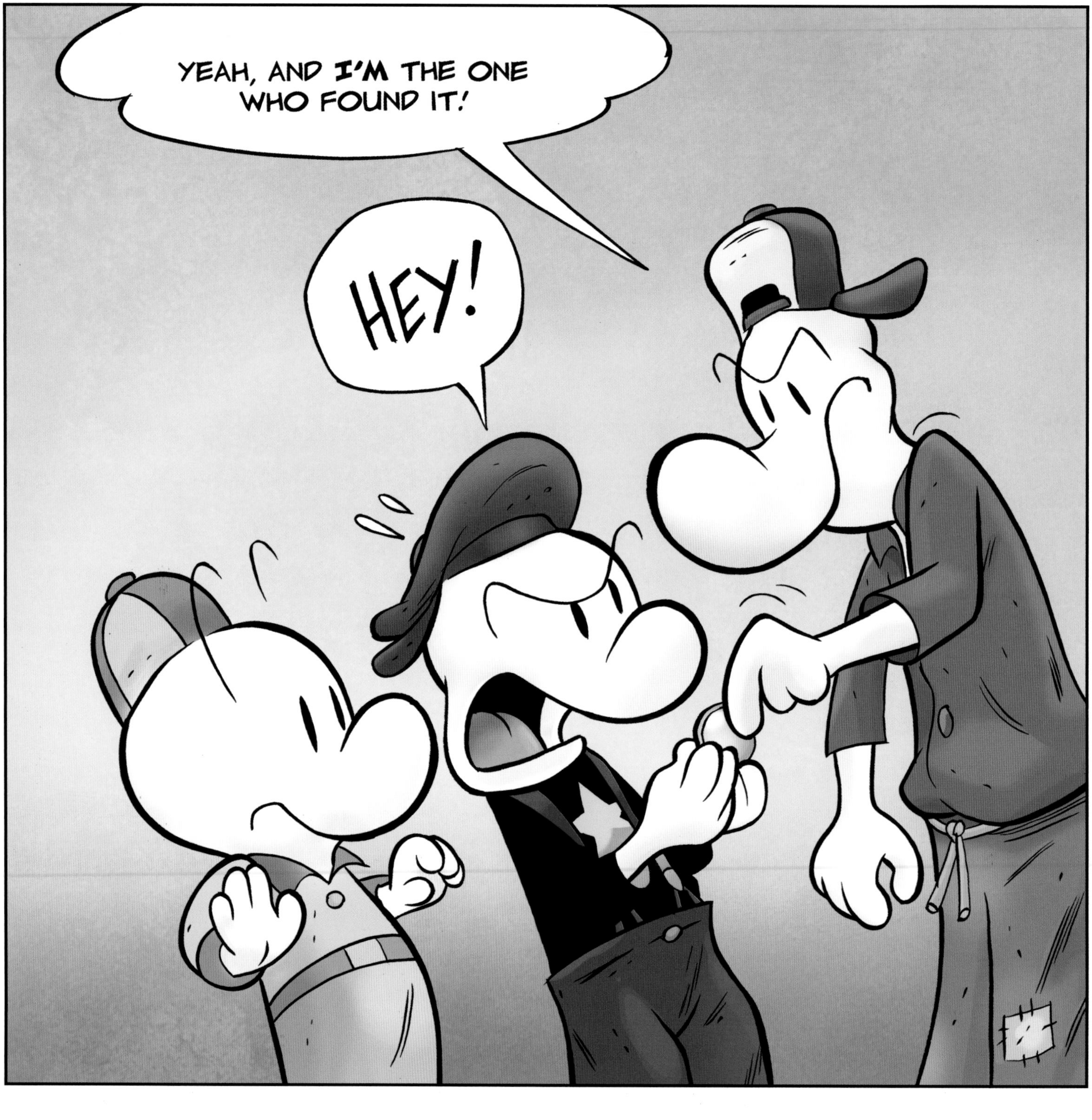
YEAH, AND **I'M** THE ONE WHO FOUND IT!
HEY!

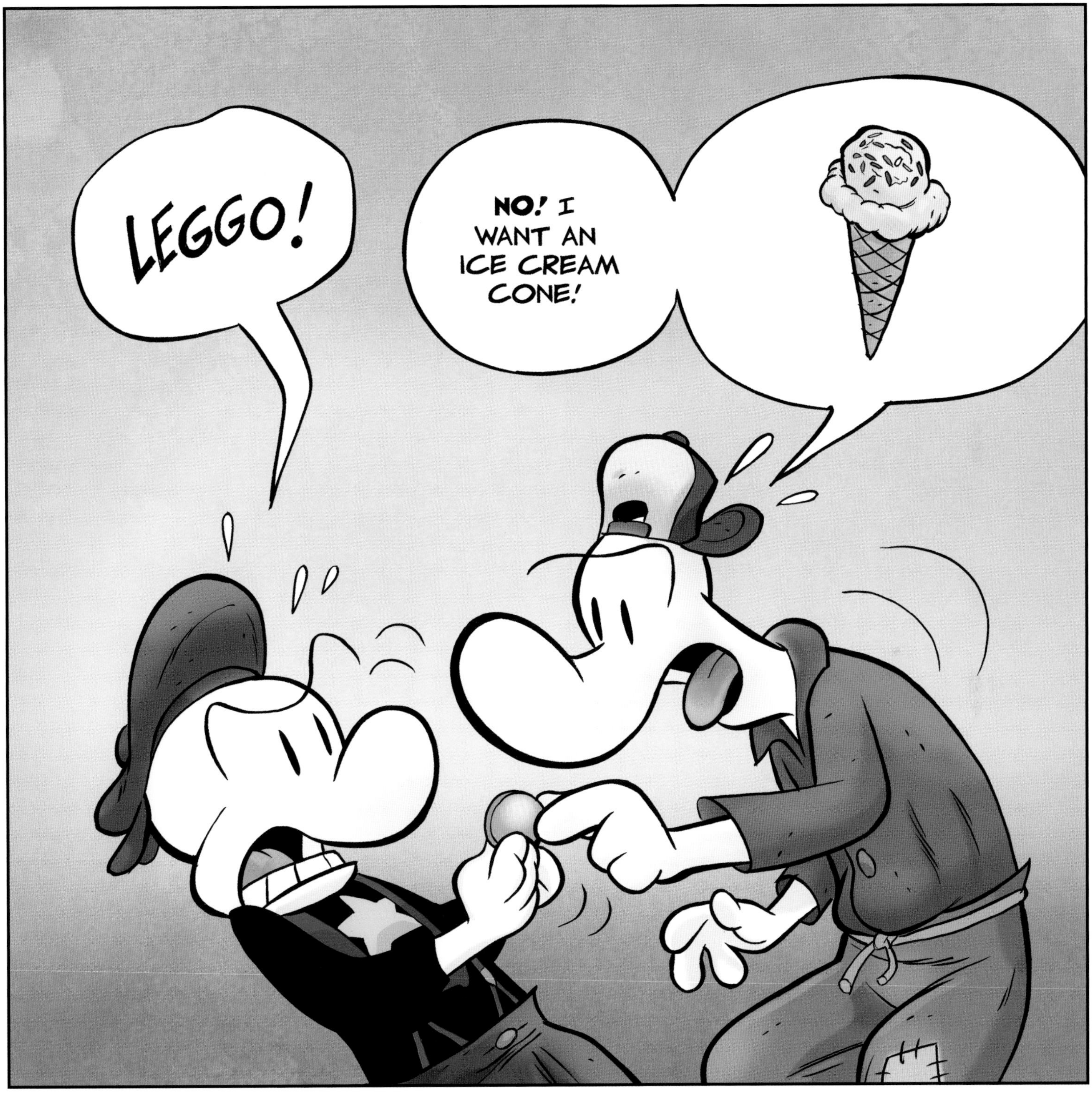
LEGGO!
NO! I WANT AN ICE CREAM CONE!

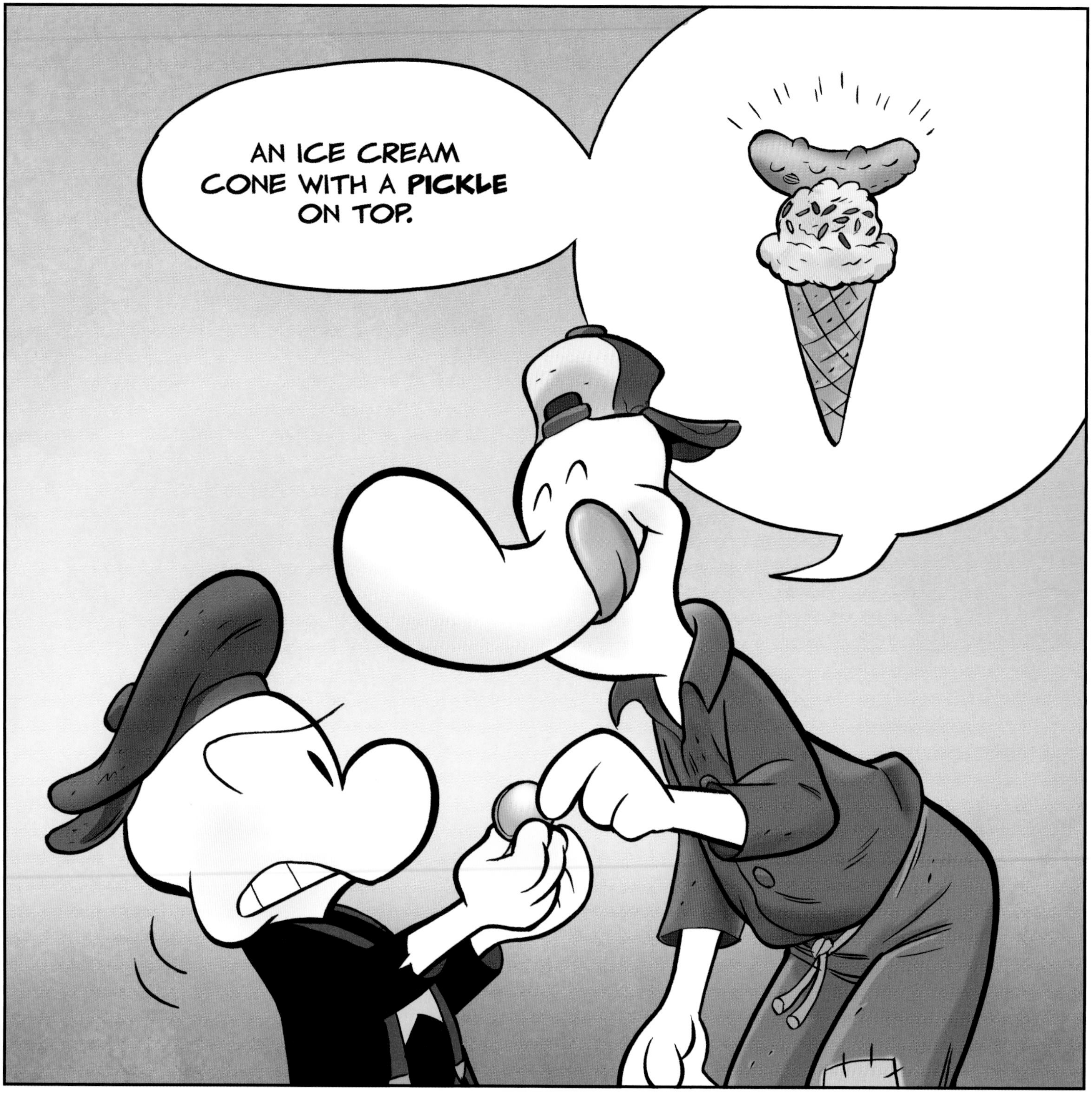
AN ICE CREAM CONE WITH A PICKLE ON TOP.

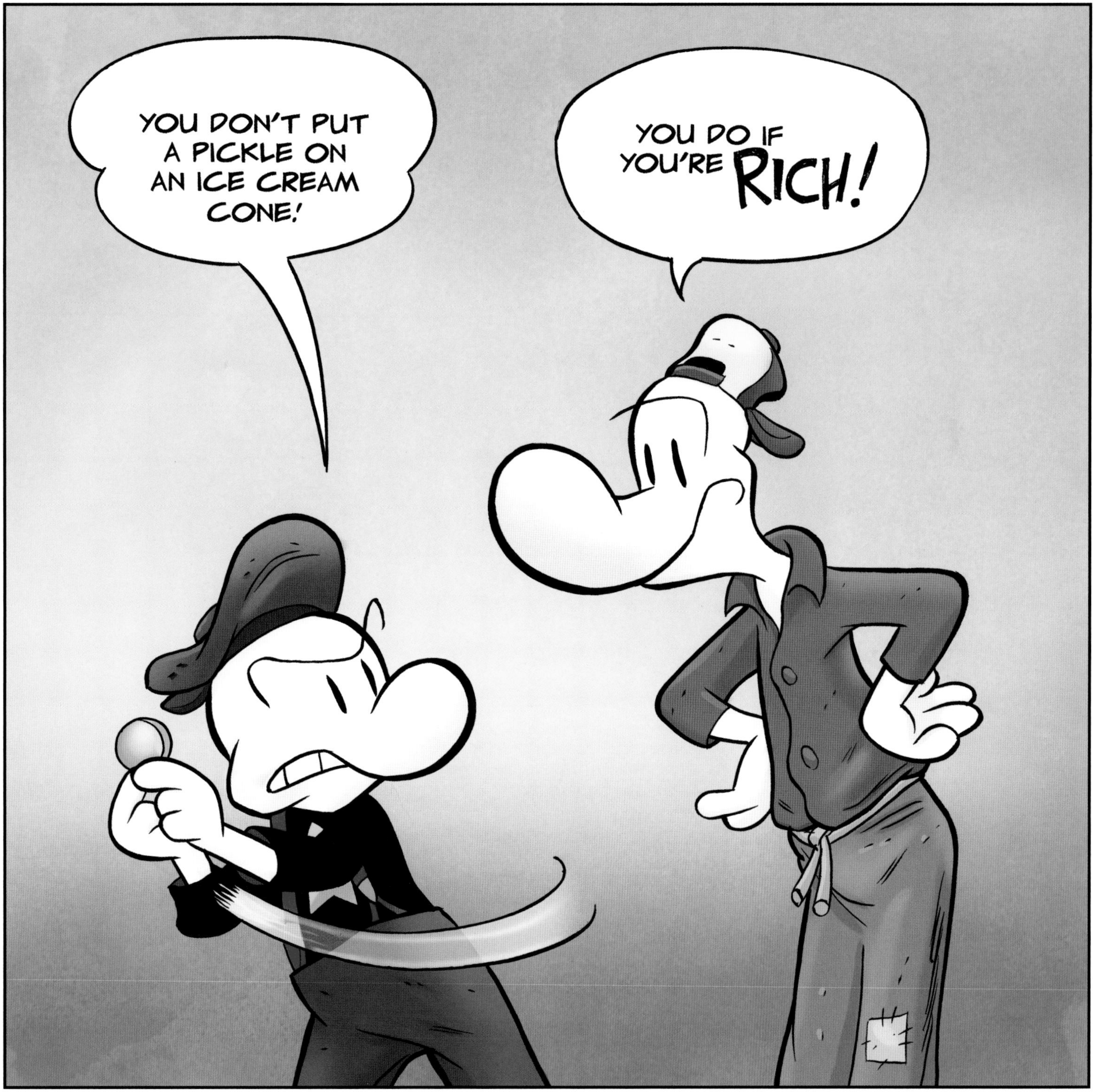
YOU DON'T PUT A PICKLE ON AN ICE CREAM CONE!
YOU DO IF YOU'RE RICH!

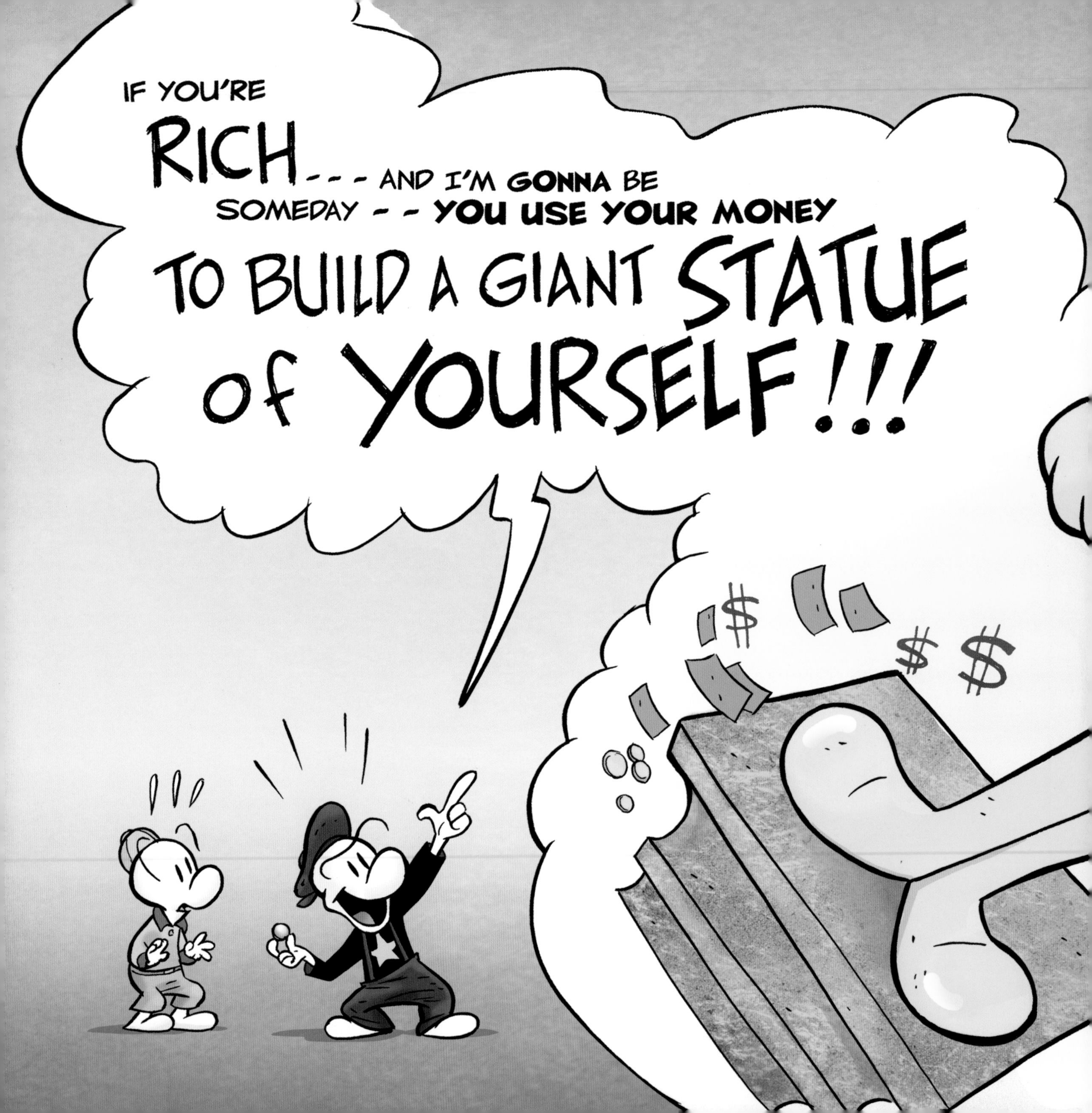
IF YOU'RE RICH--- AND I'M GONNA BE SOMEDAY -- YOU USE YOUR MONEY TO BUILD A GIANT STATUE of YOURSELF!!!

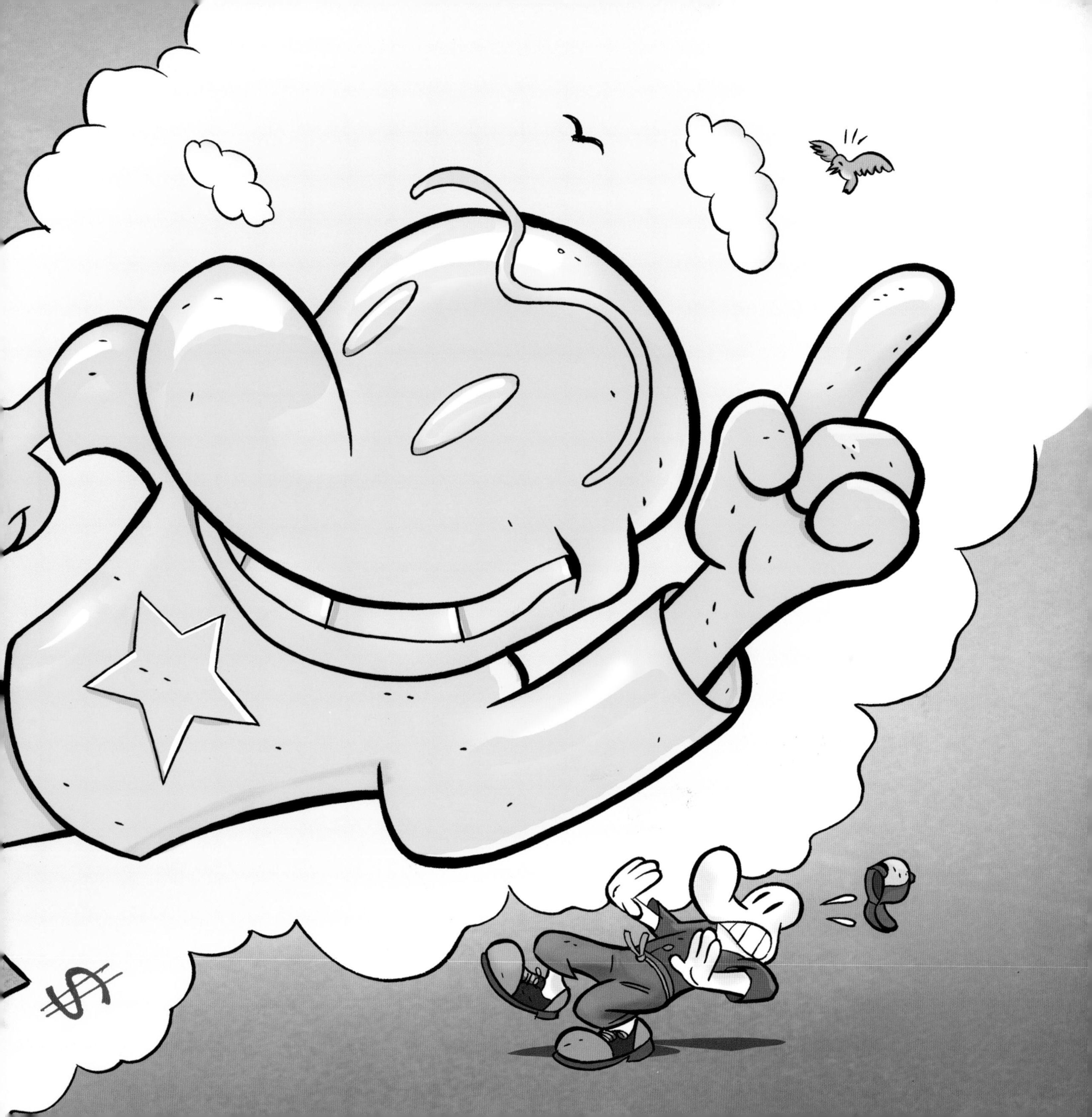

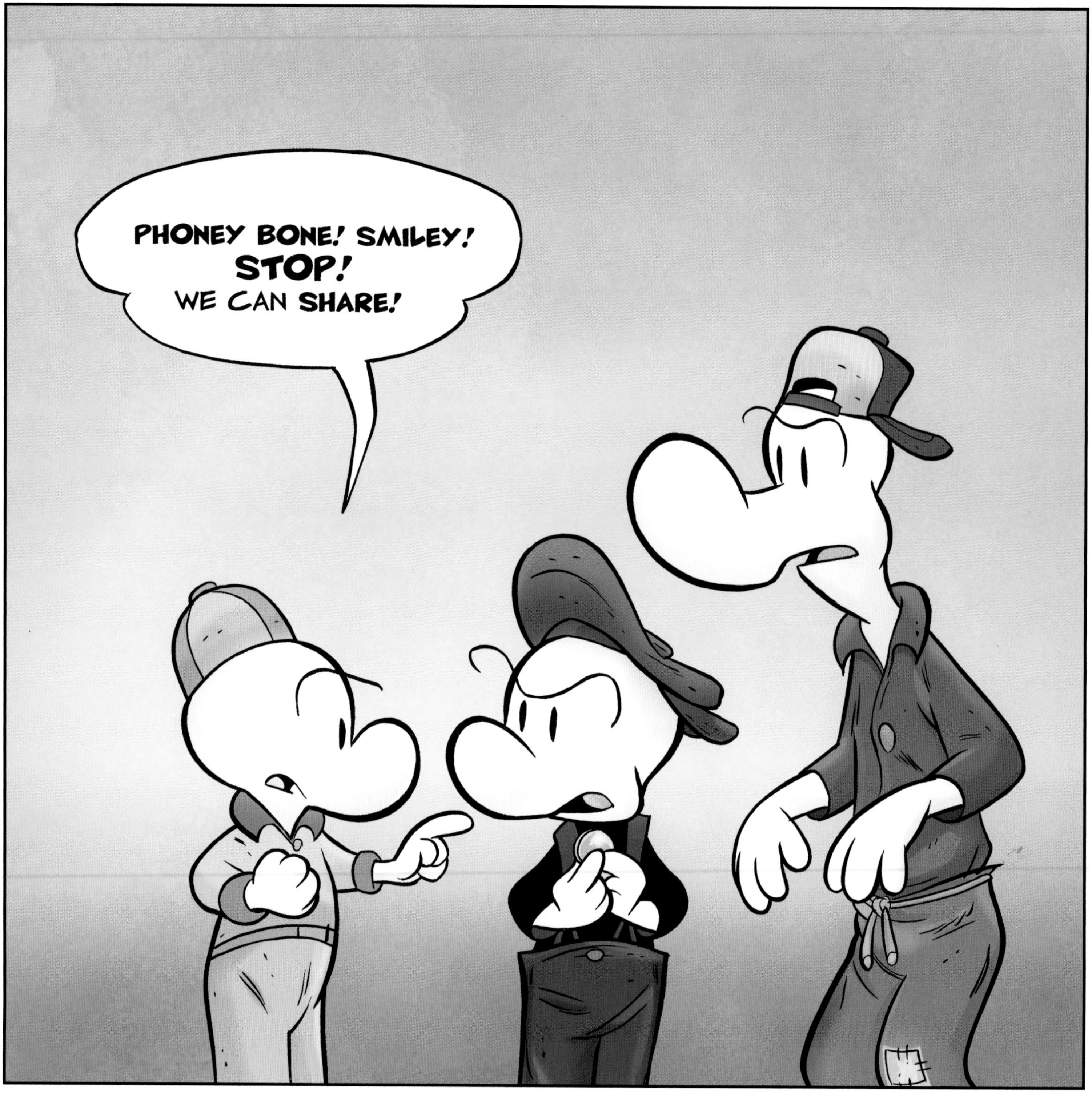
PHONEY BONE! SMILEY! STOP! WE CAN SHARE!

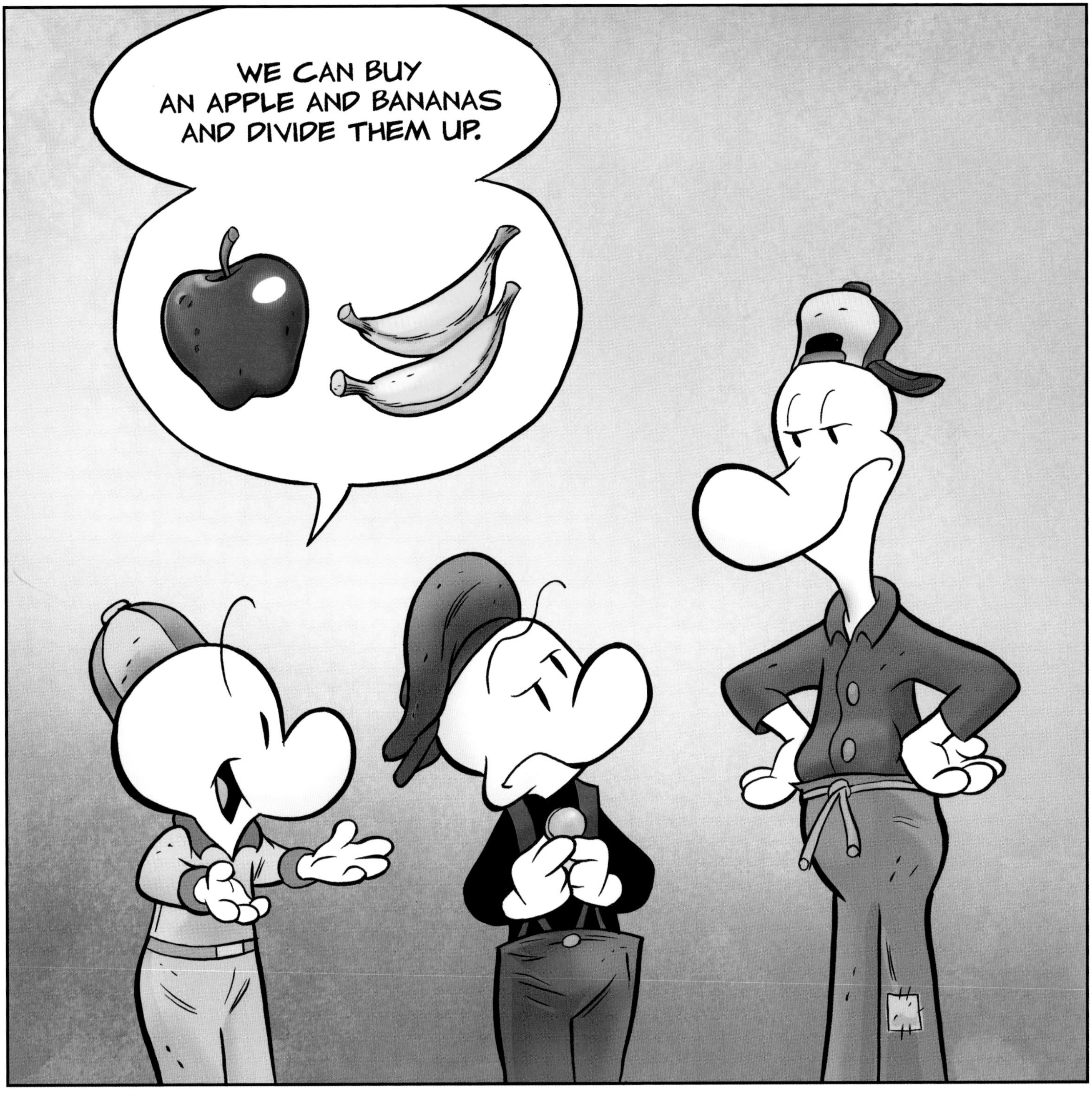
WE CAN BUY AN APPLE AND BANANAS AND DIVIDE THEM UP.

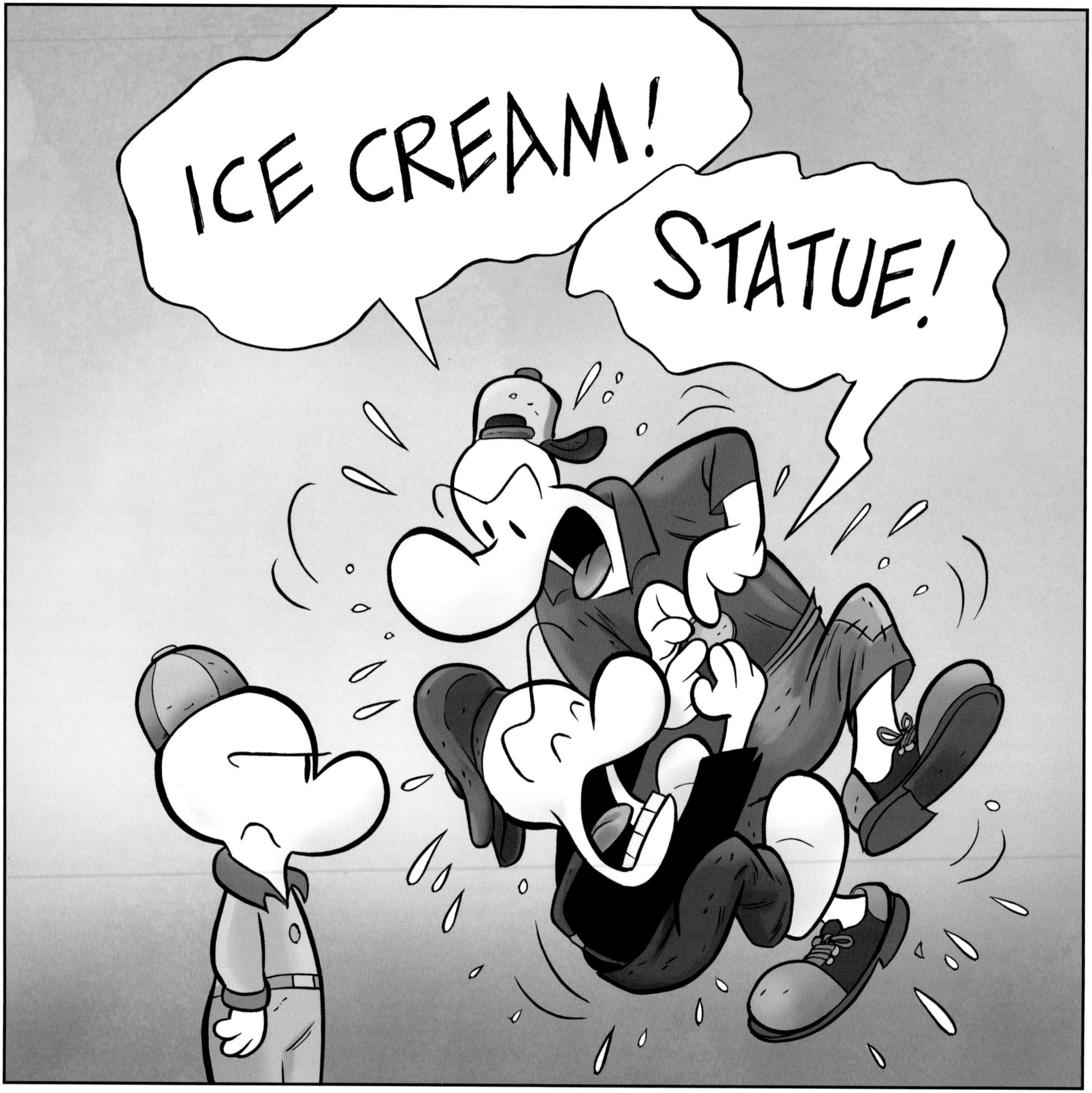
ICE CREAM!
STATUE!

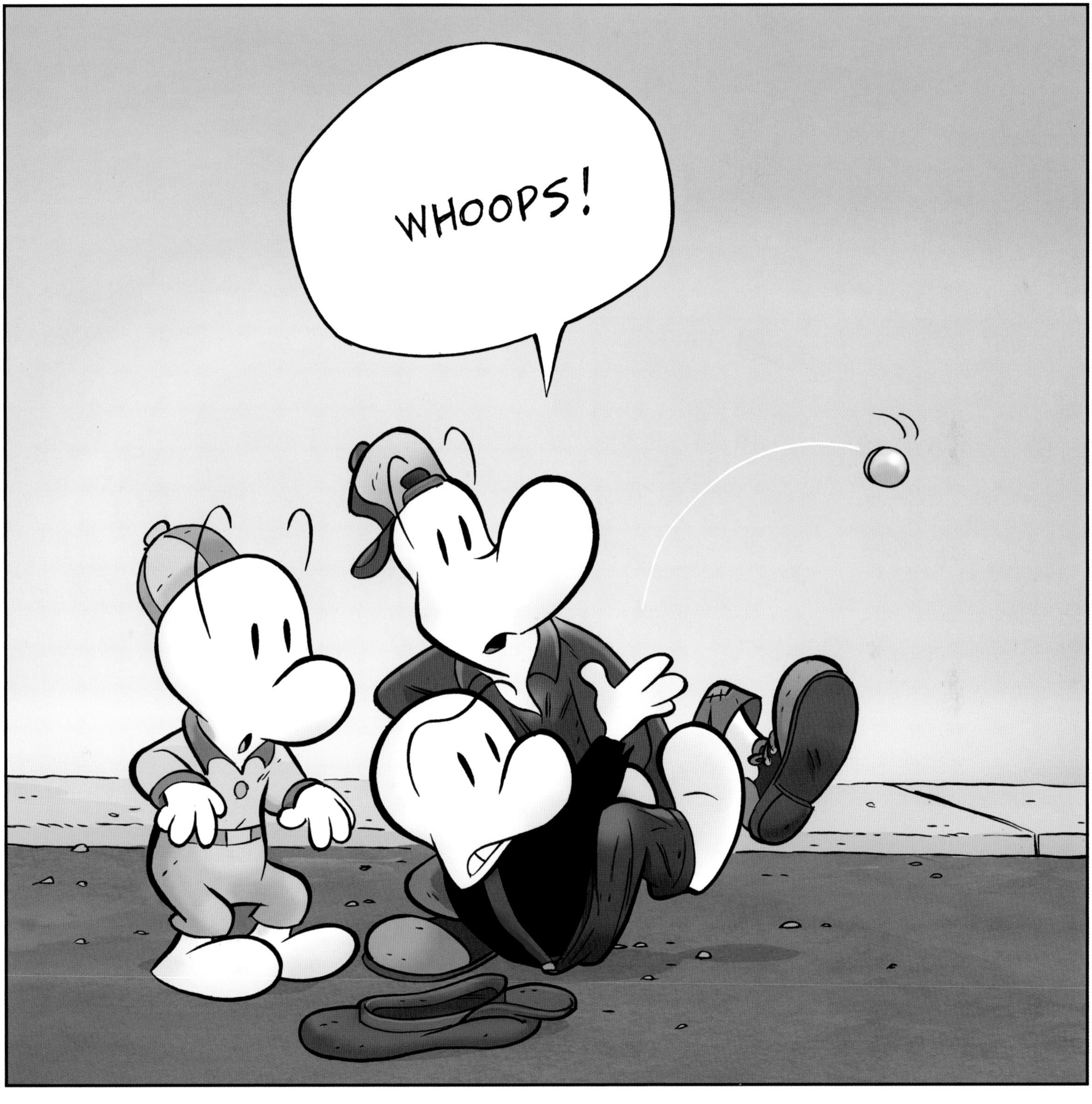
WHOOPS!

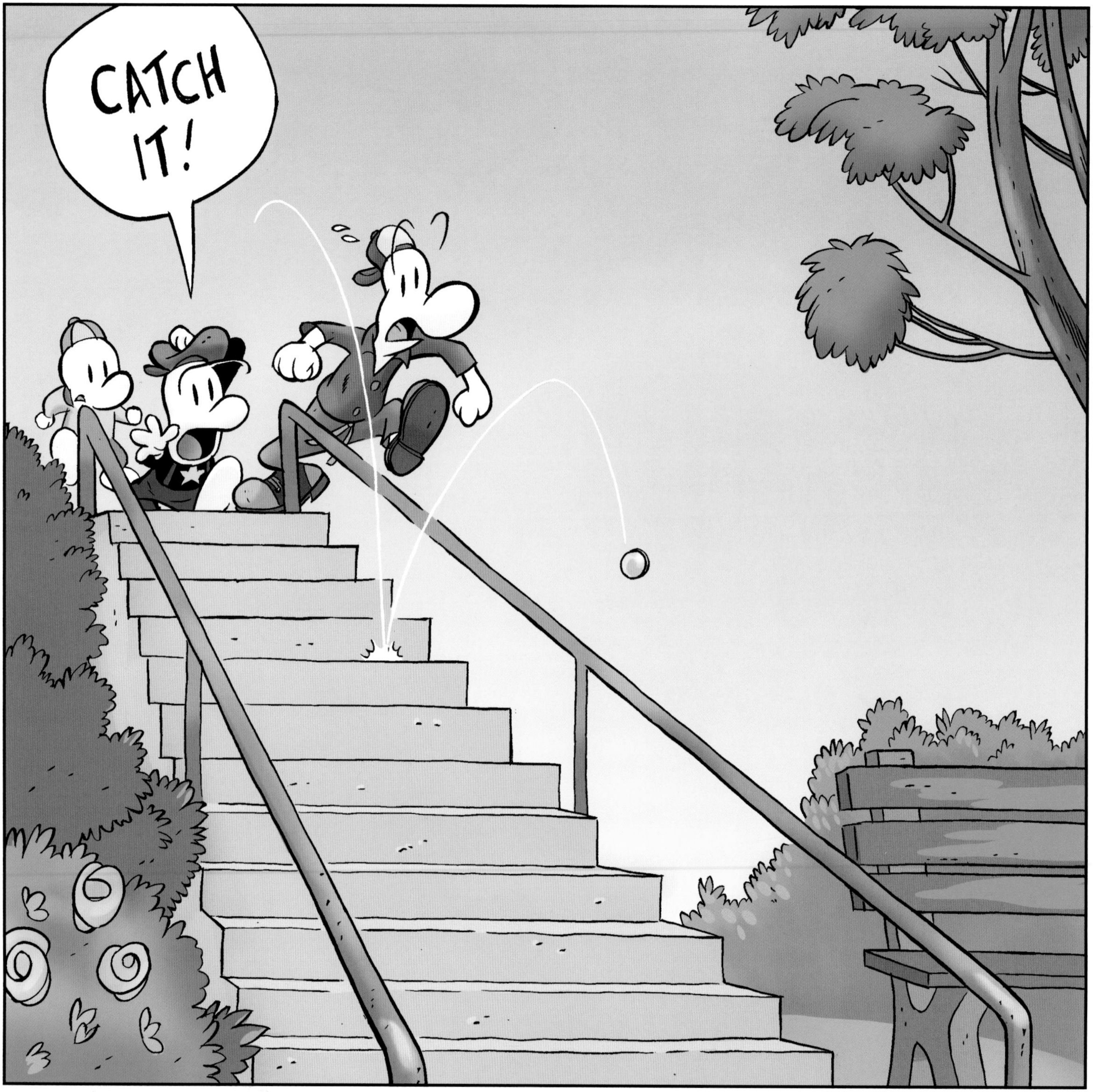
CATCH IT!

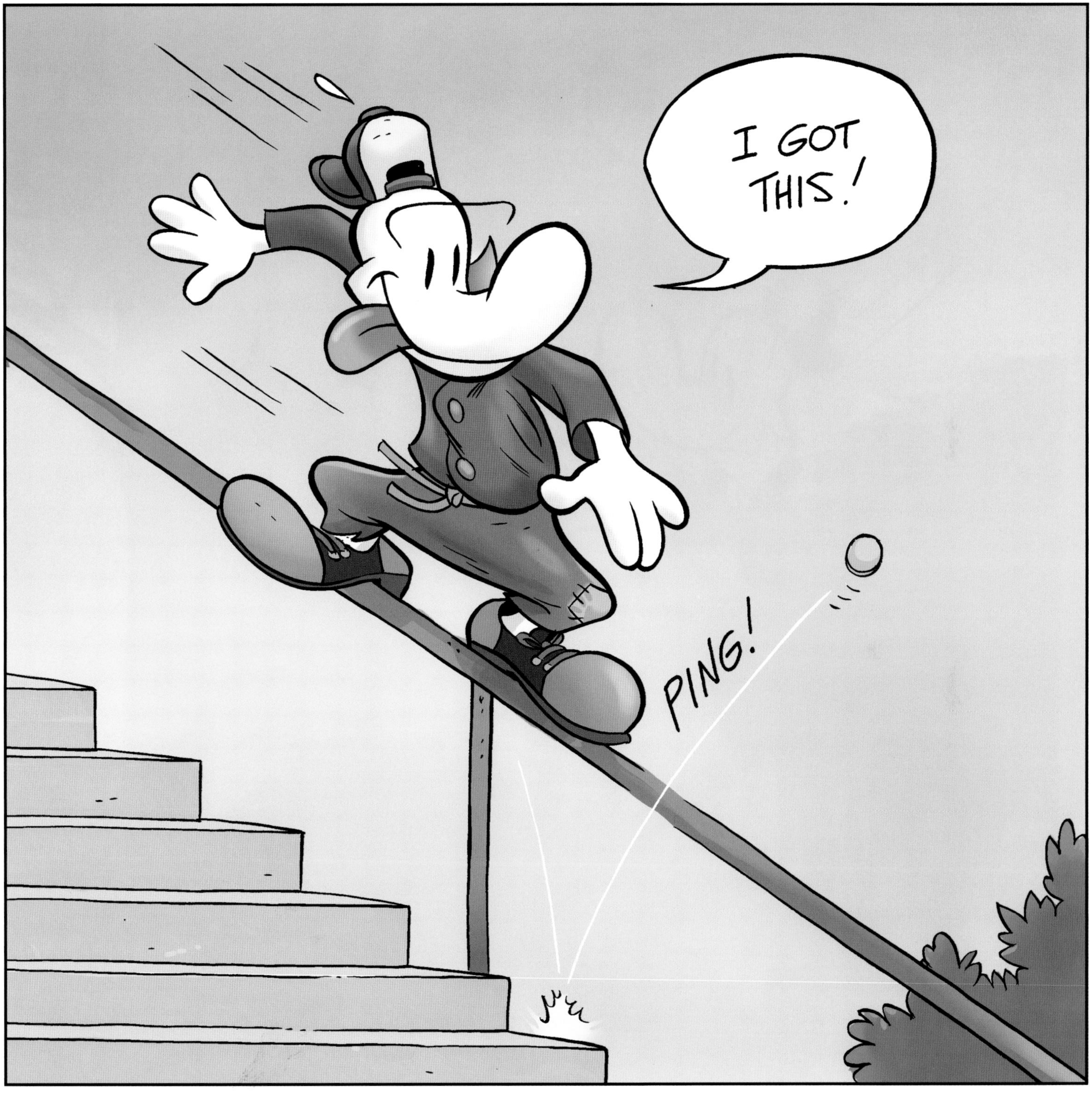
I GOT THIS!
PING!

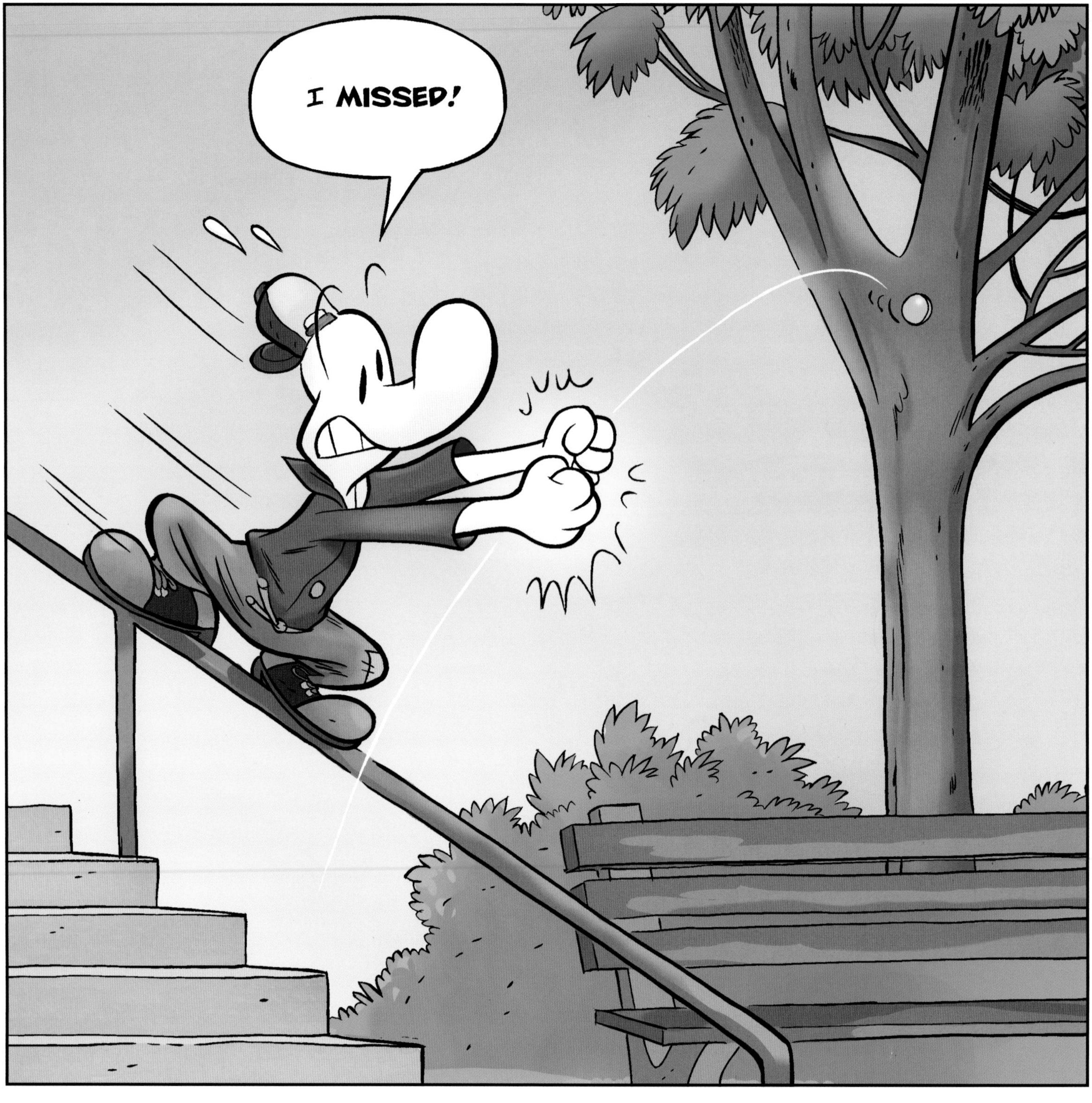
I MISSED!

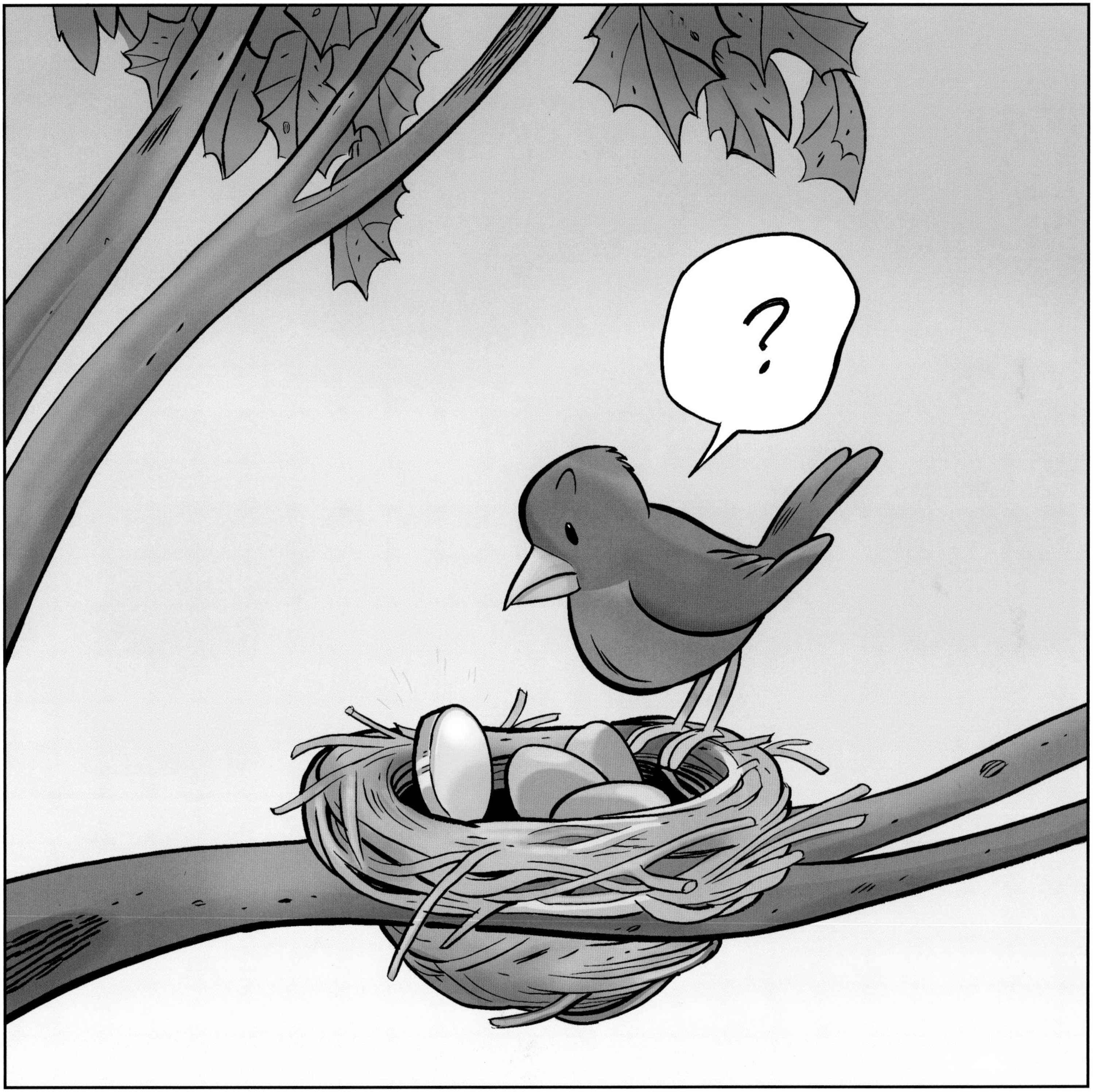
?

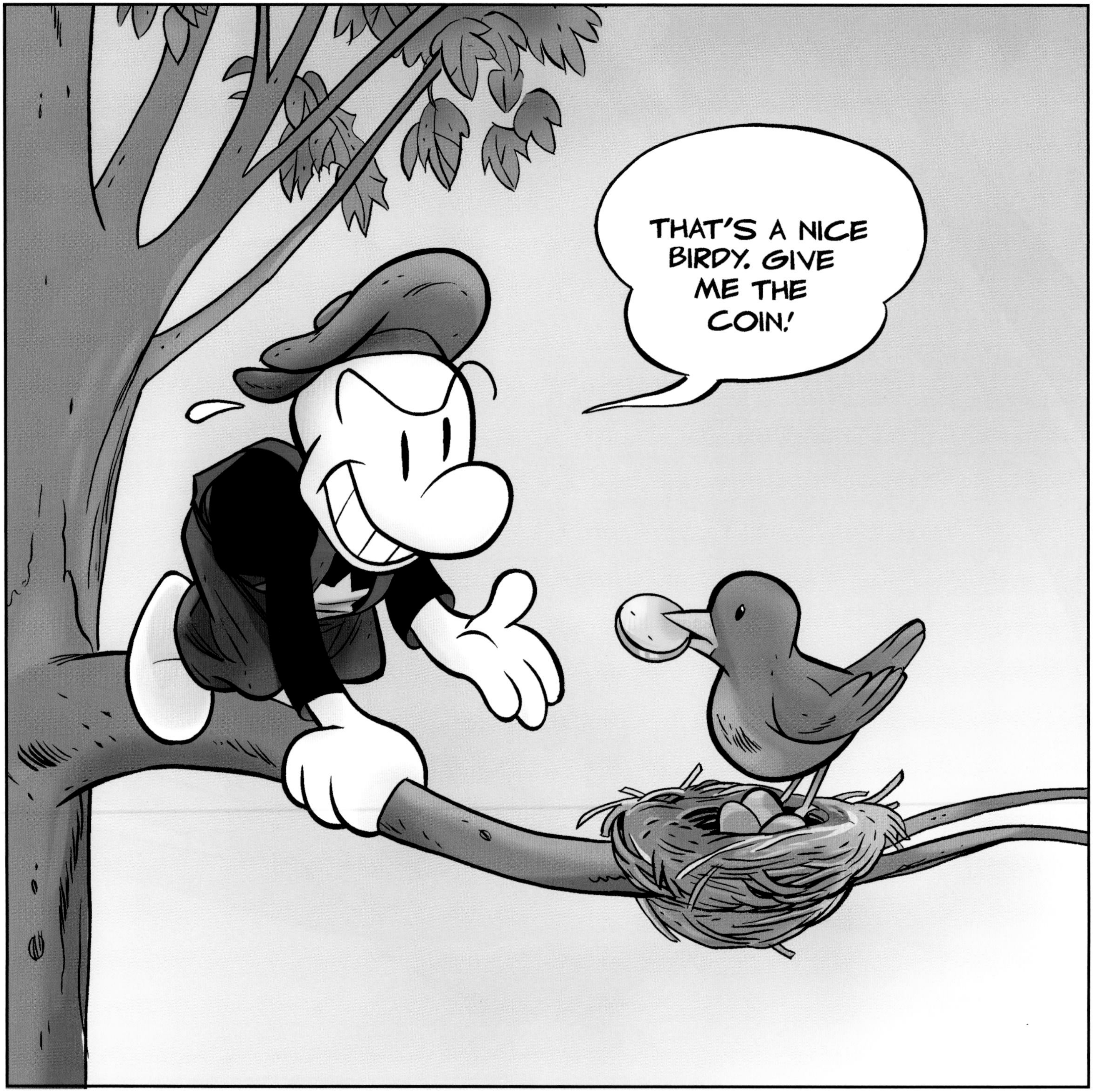
THAT'S A NICE BIRDY. GIVE ME THE COIN!

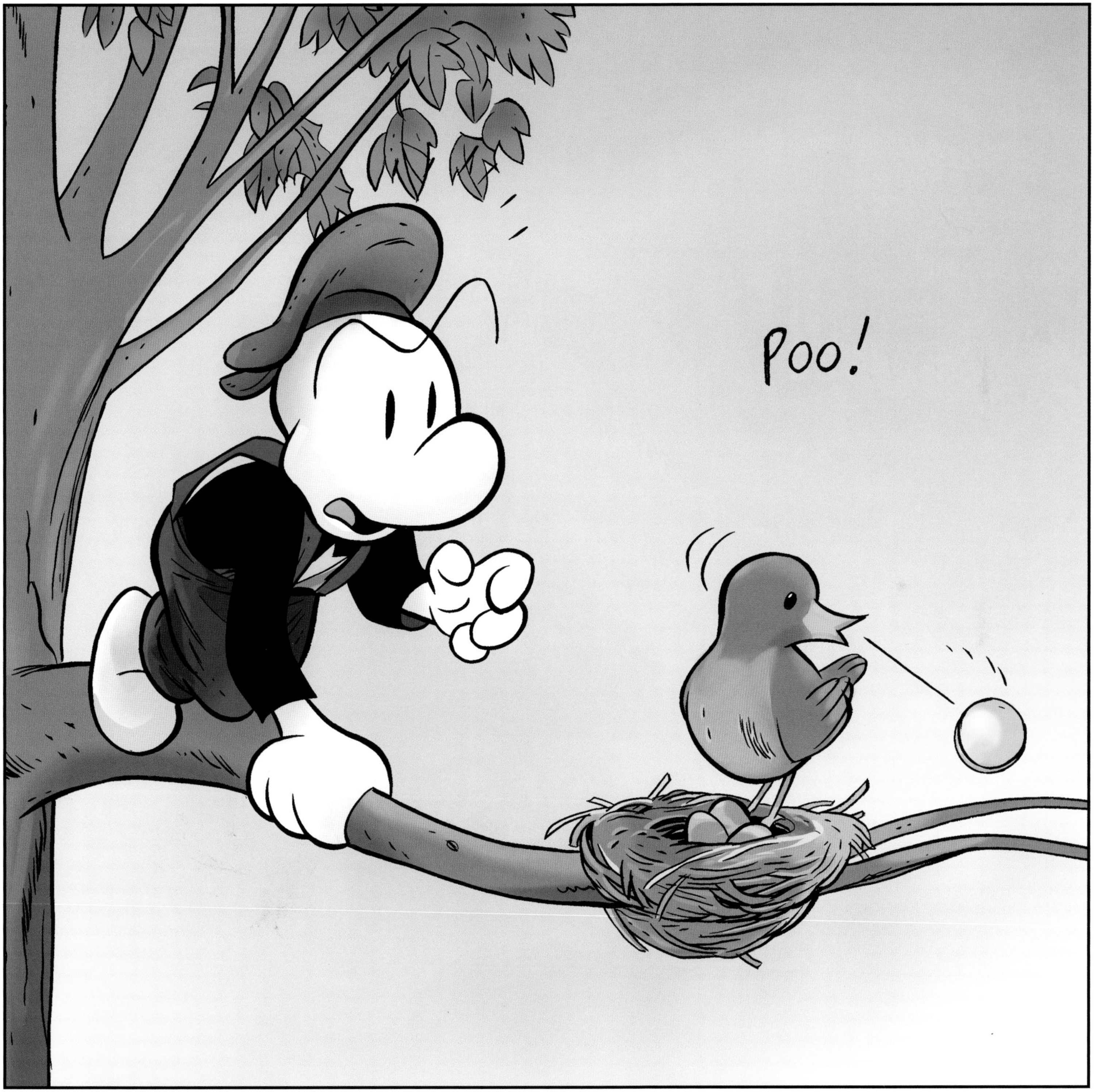
POO!

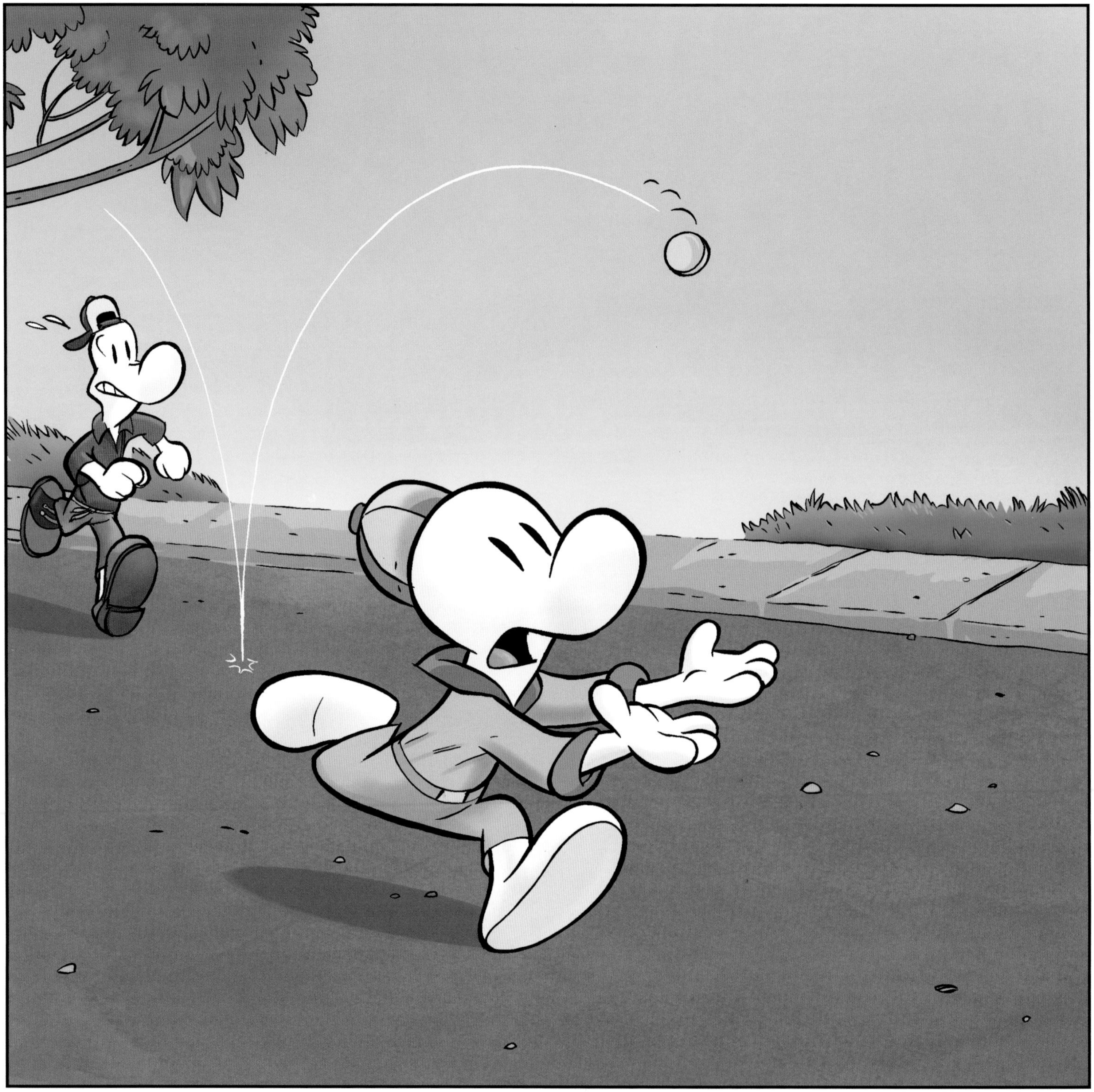

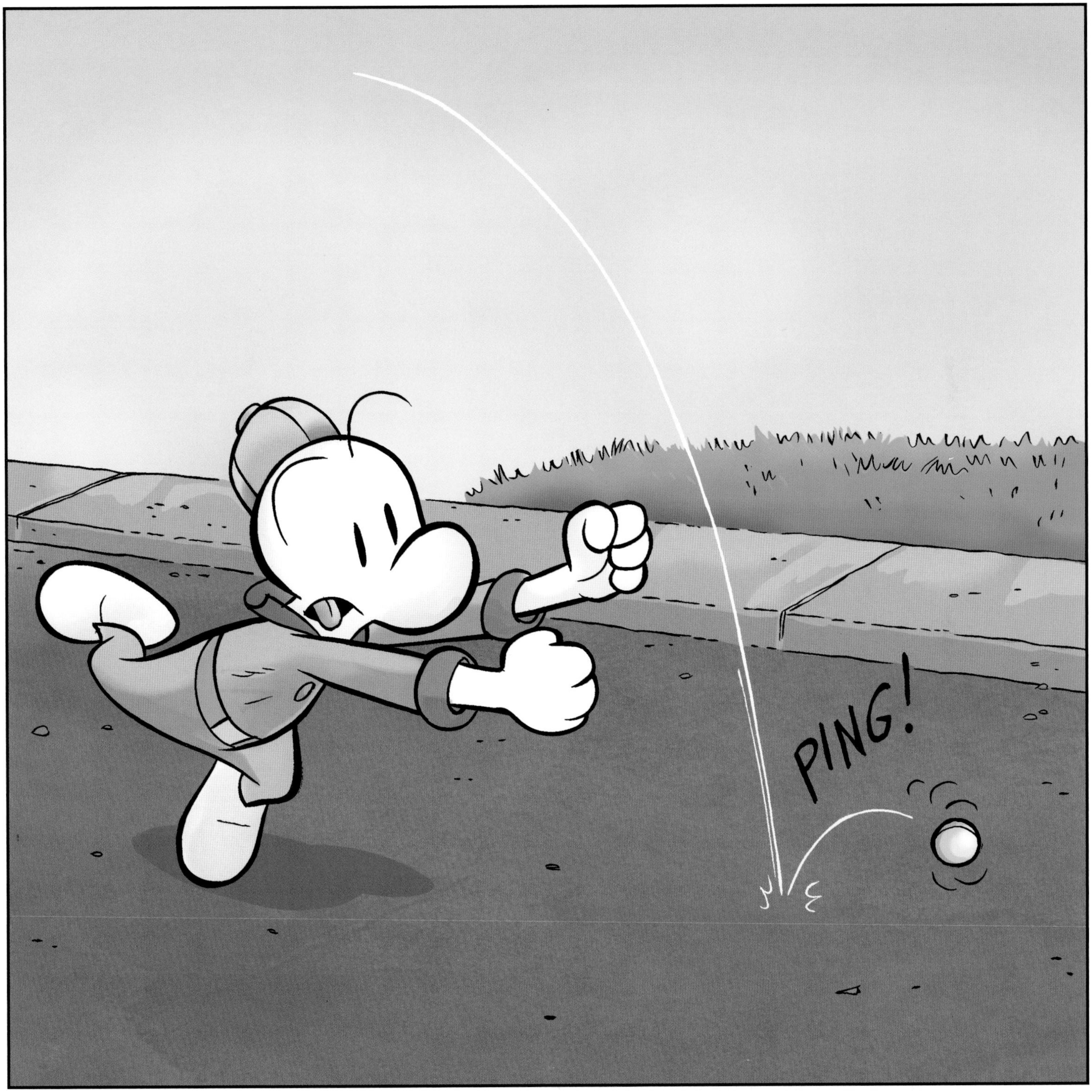
PING!

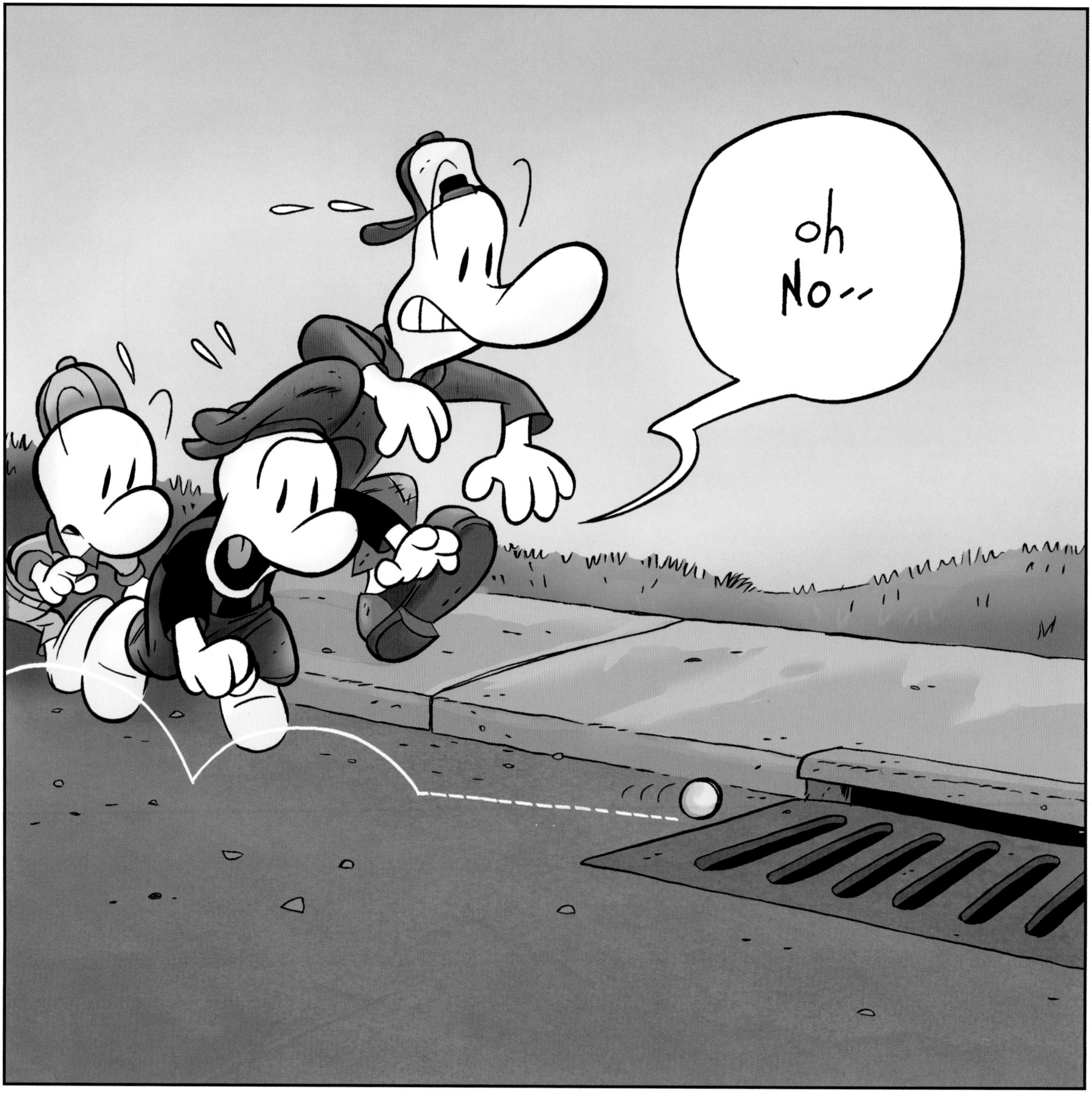
oh No...

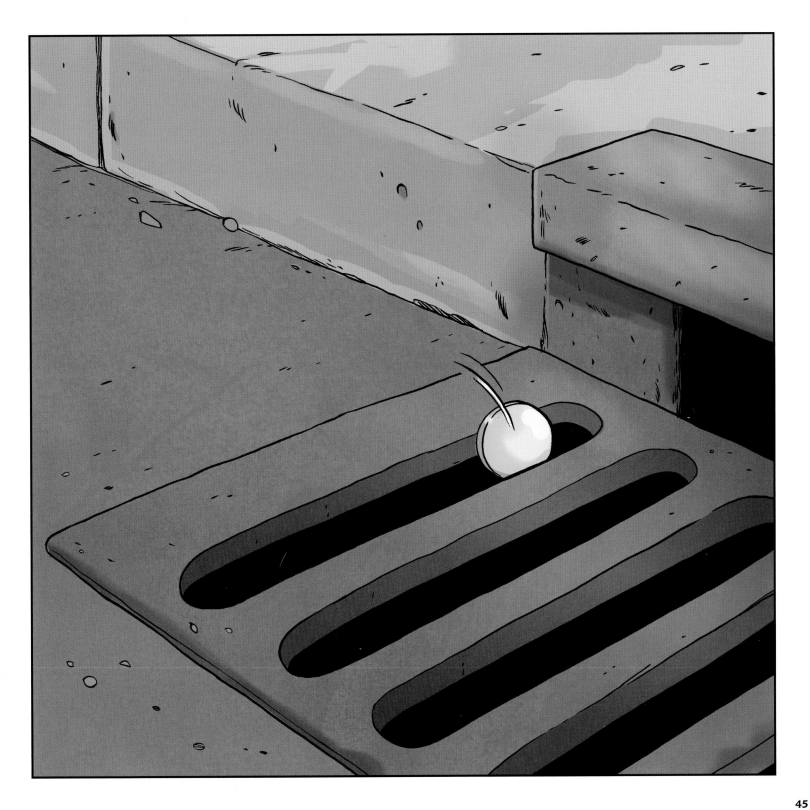

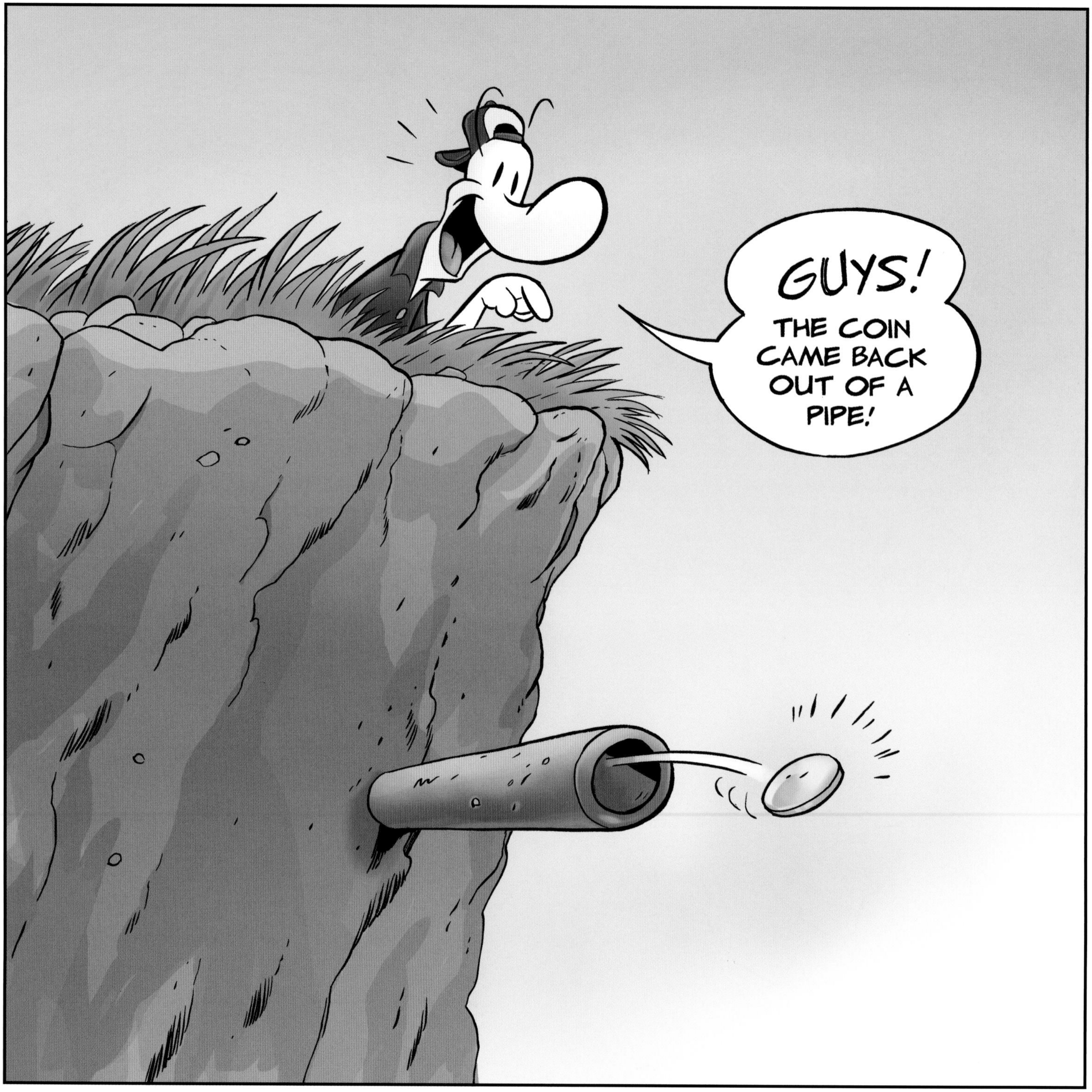
GUYS!
THE COIN CAME BACK OUT OF A PIPE!

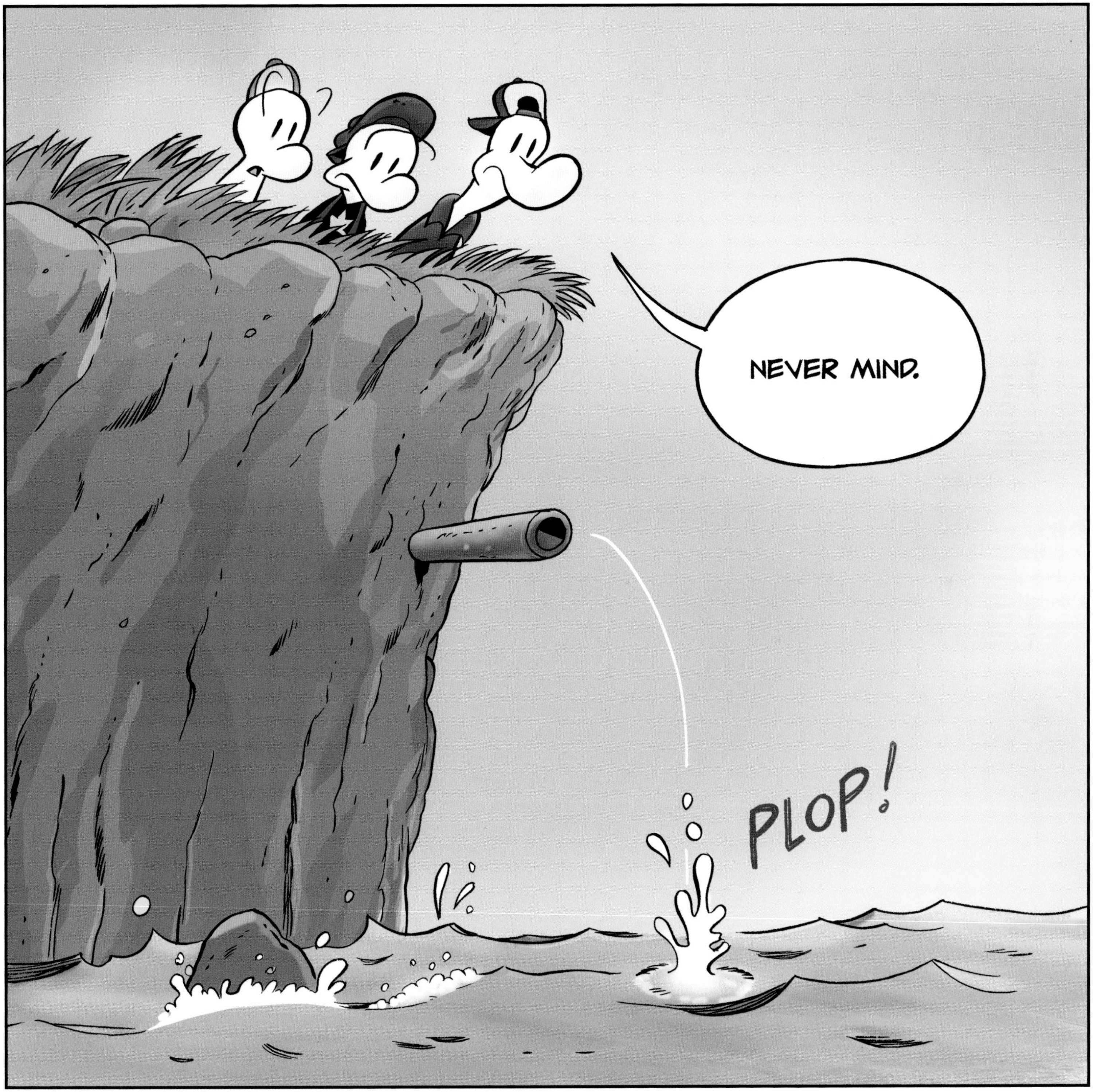
NEVER MIND.
PLOP!

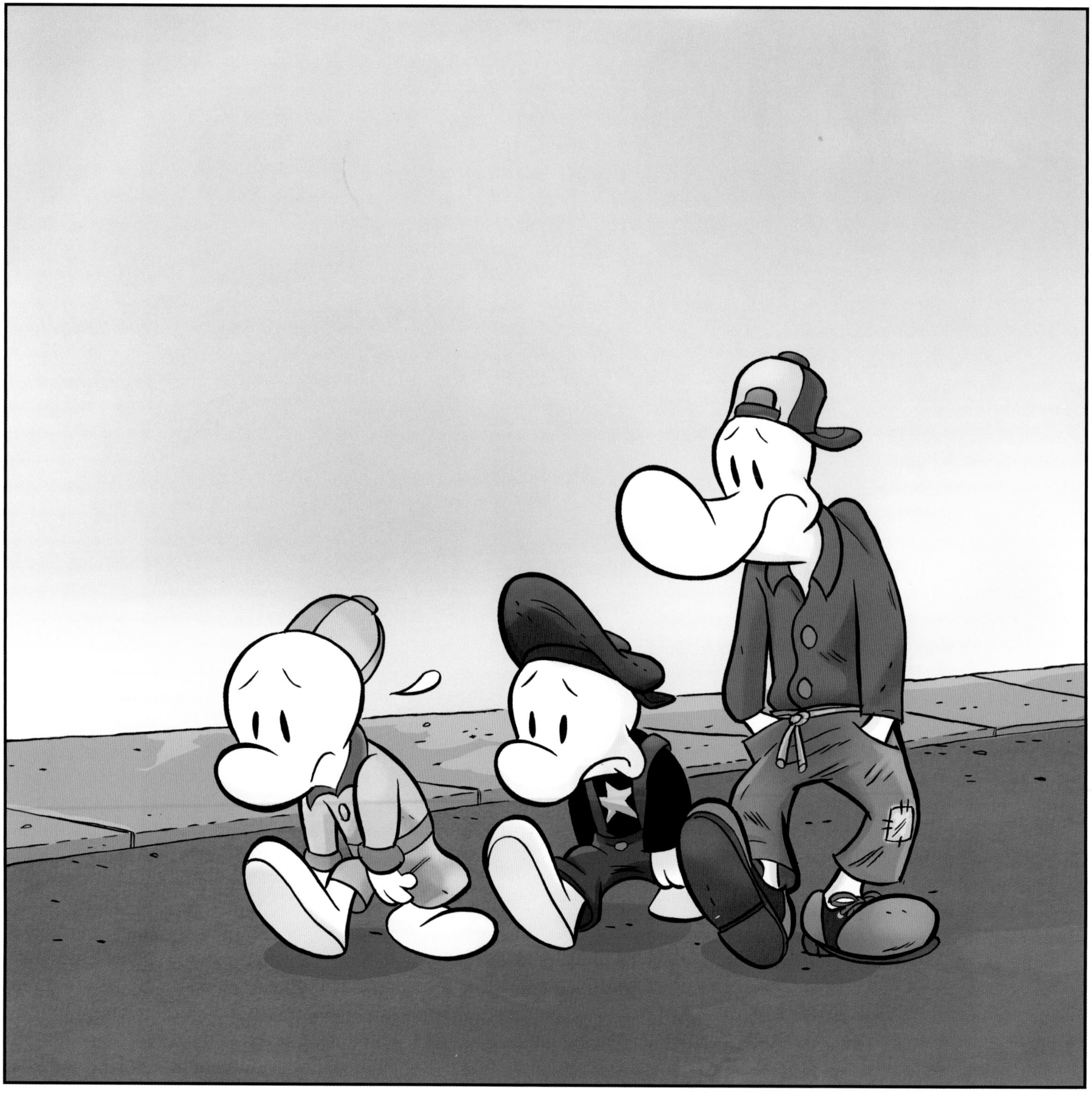

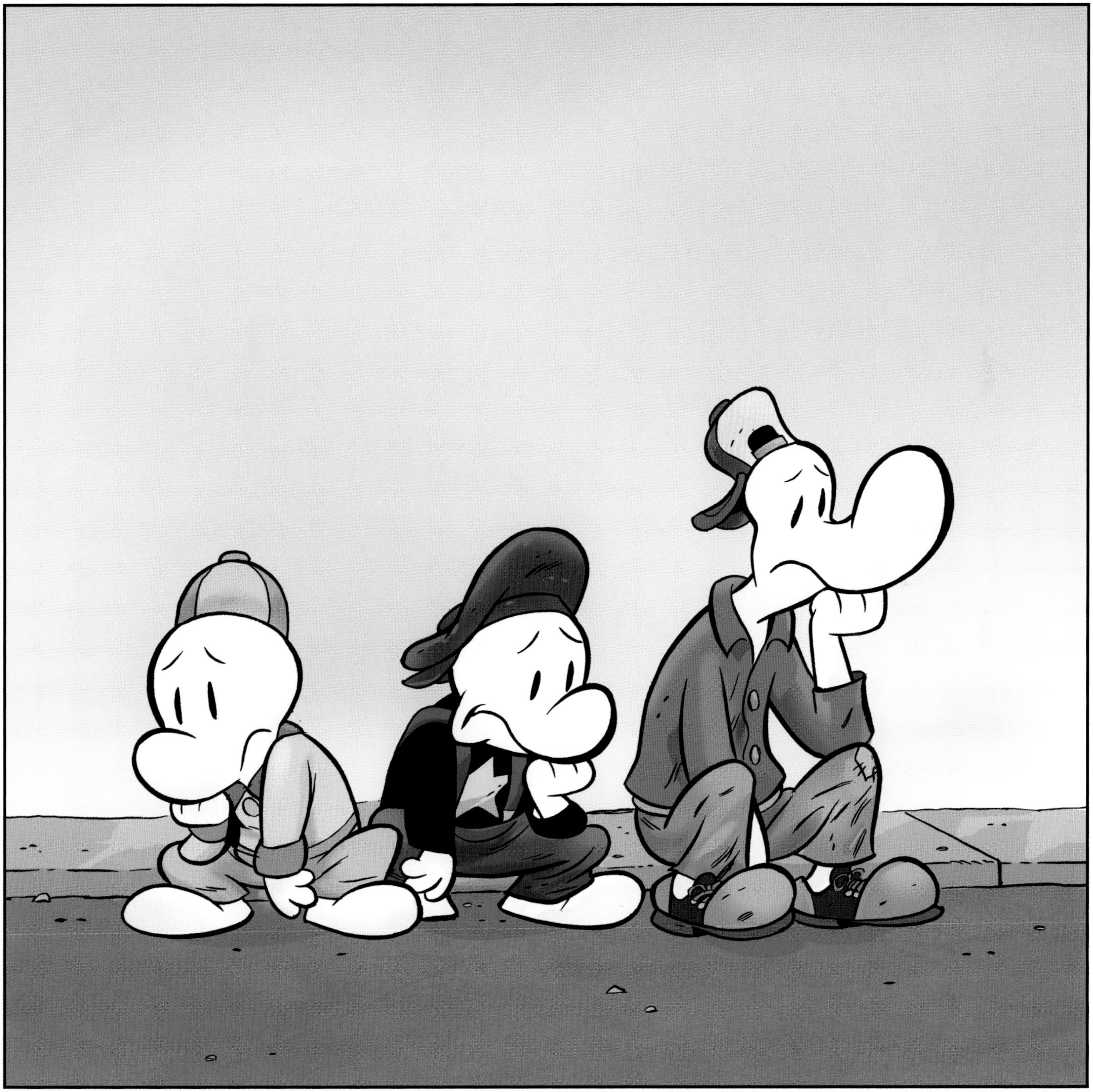

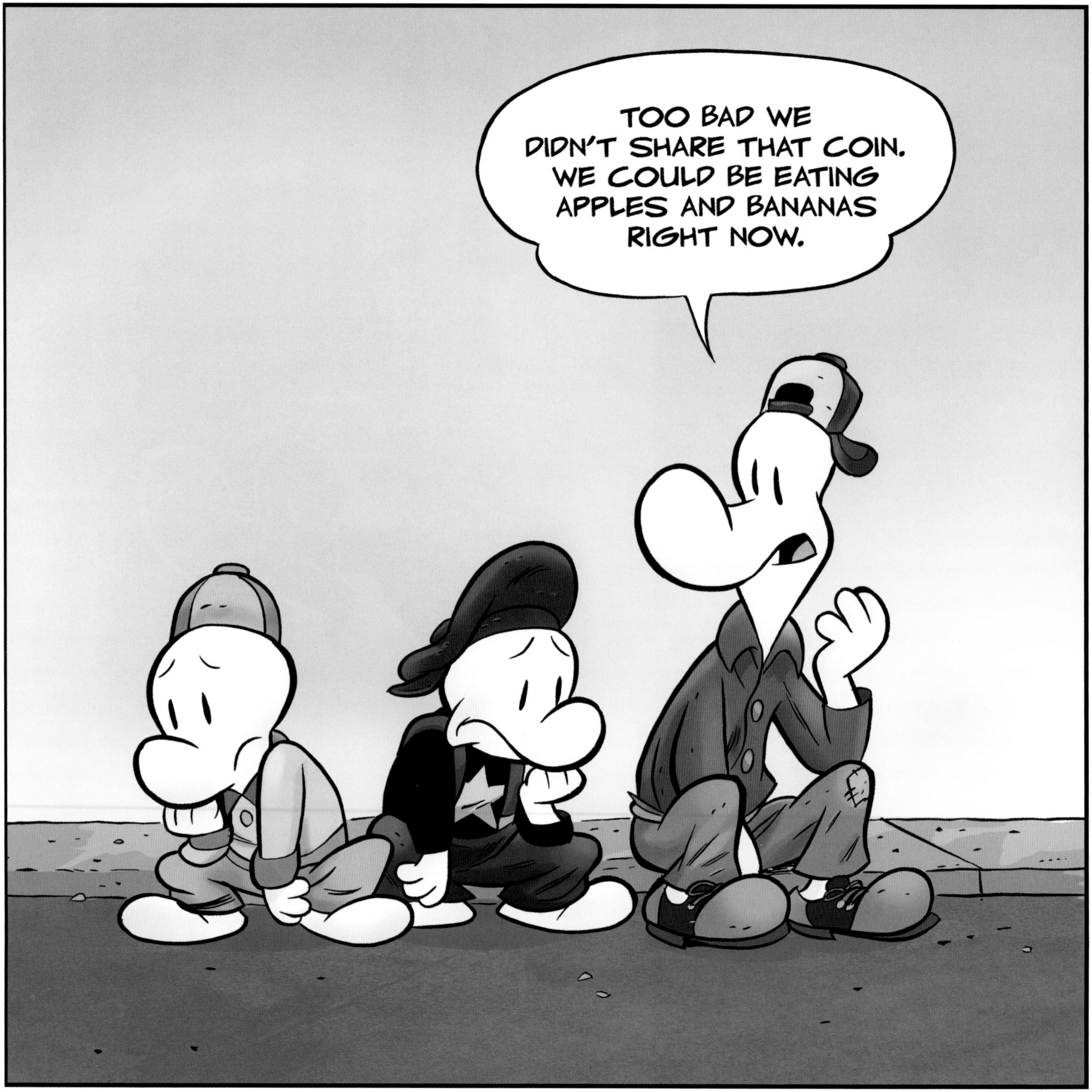
TOO BAD WE DIDN'T SHARE THAT COIN. WE COULD BE EATING APPLES AND BANANAS RIGHT NOW.

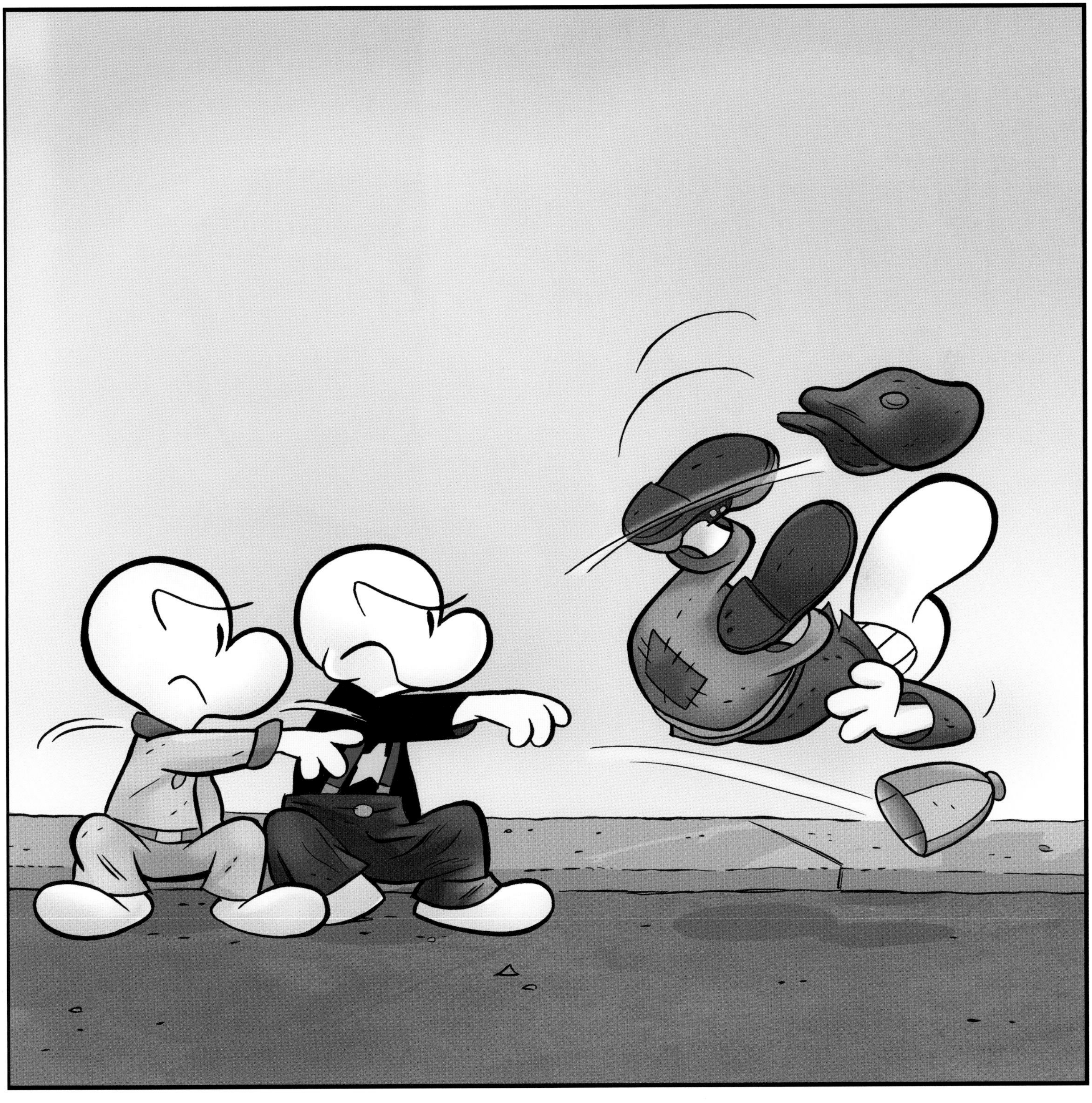

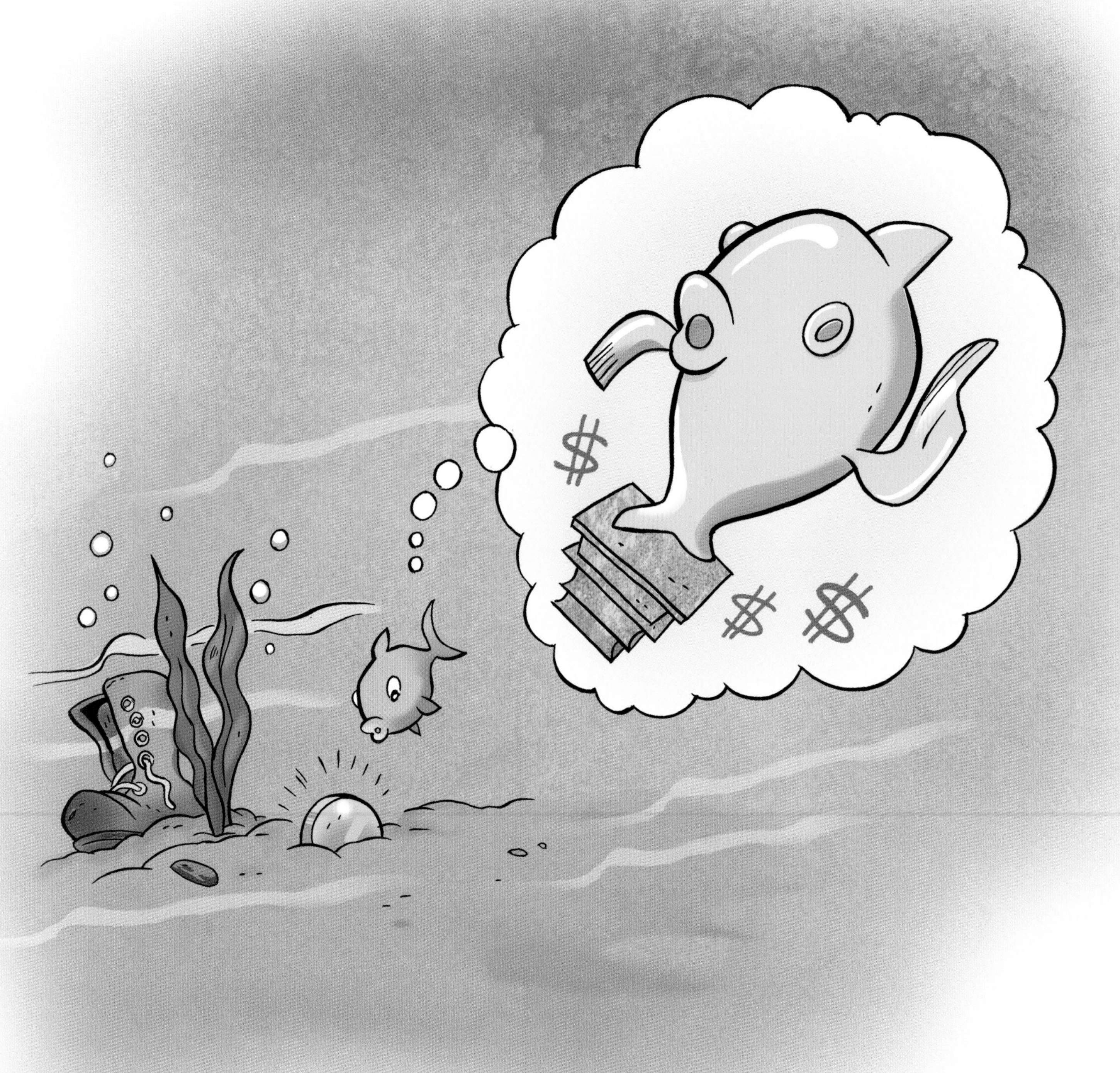
$
$ $

The End

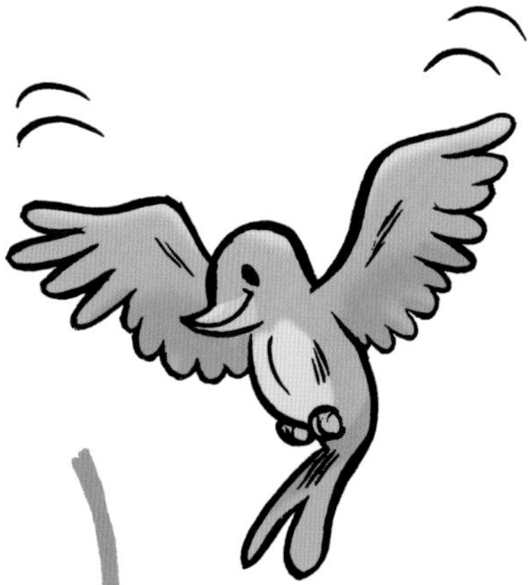

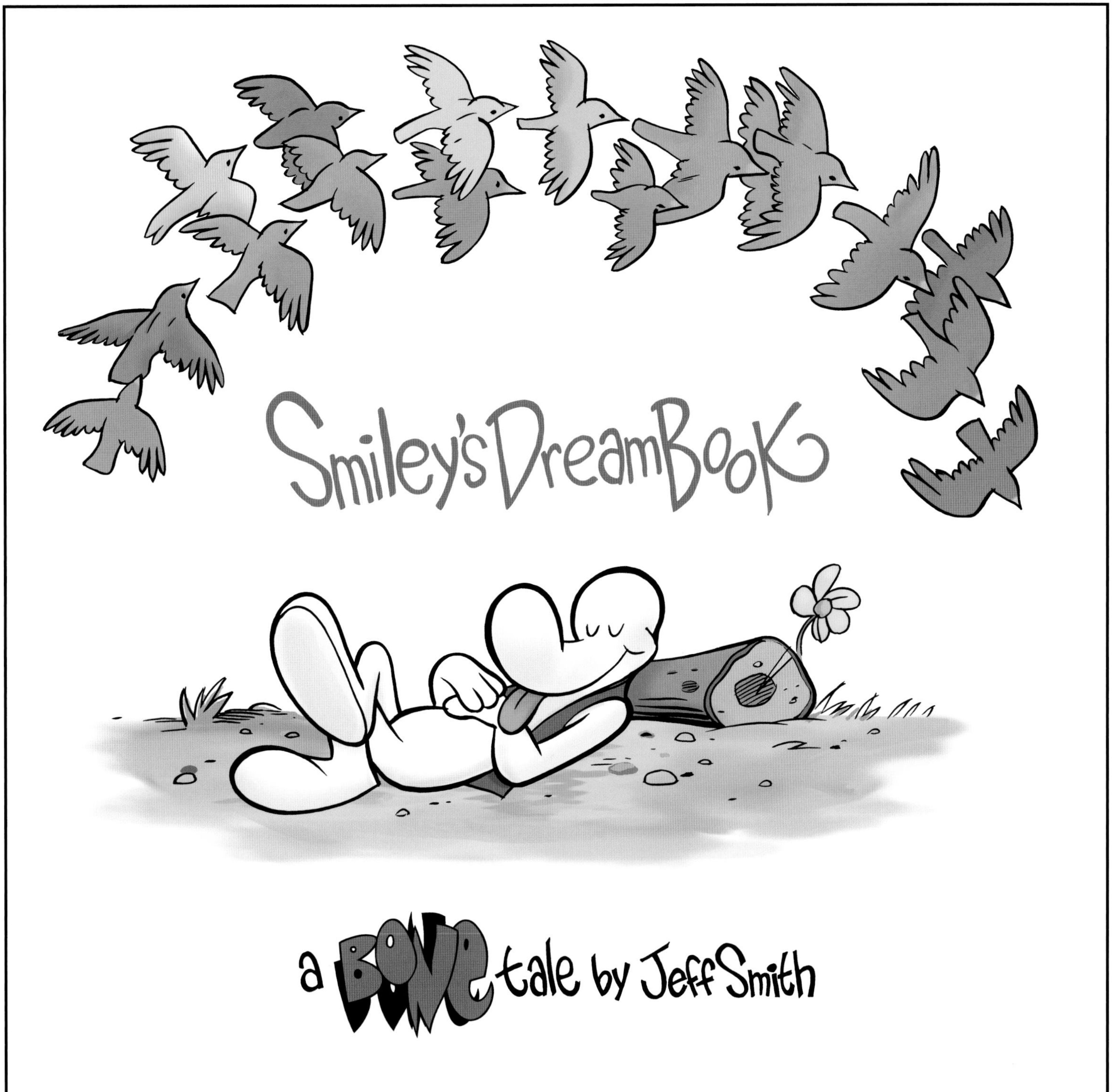
Smiley's Dream Book
a BONE tale by Jeff Smith

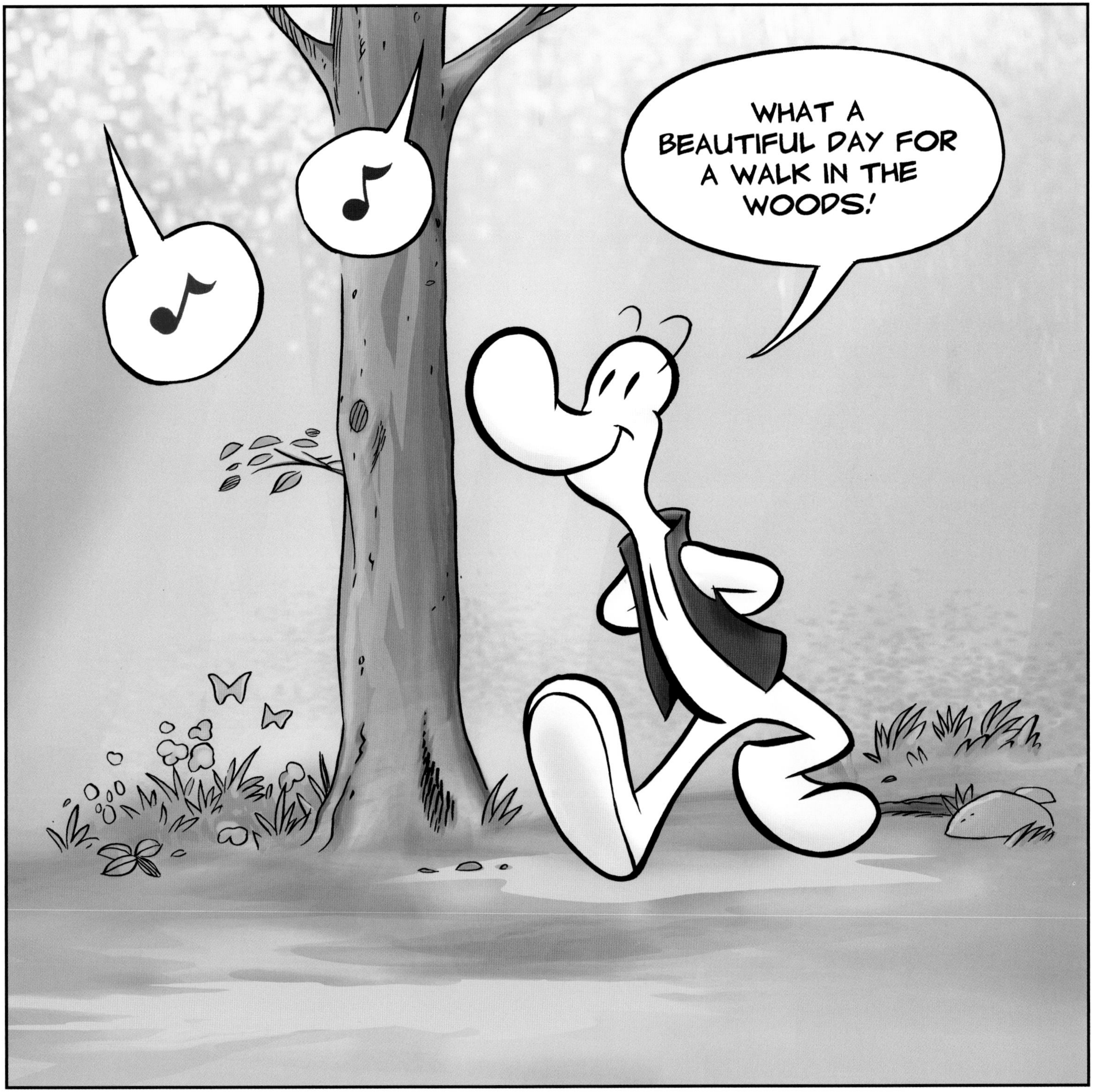
WHAT A BEAUTIFUL DAY FOR A WALK IN THE WOODS!

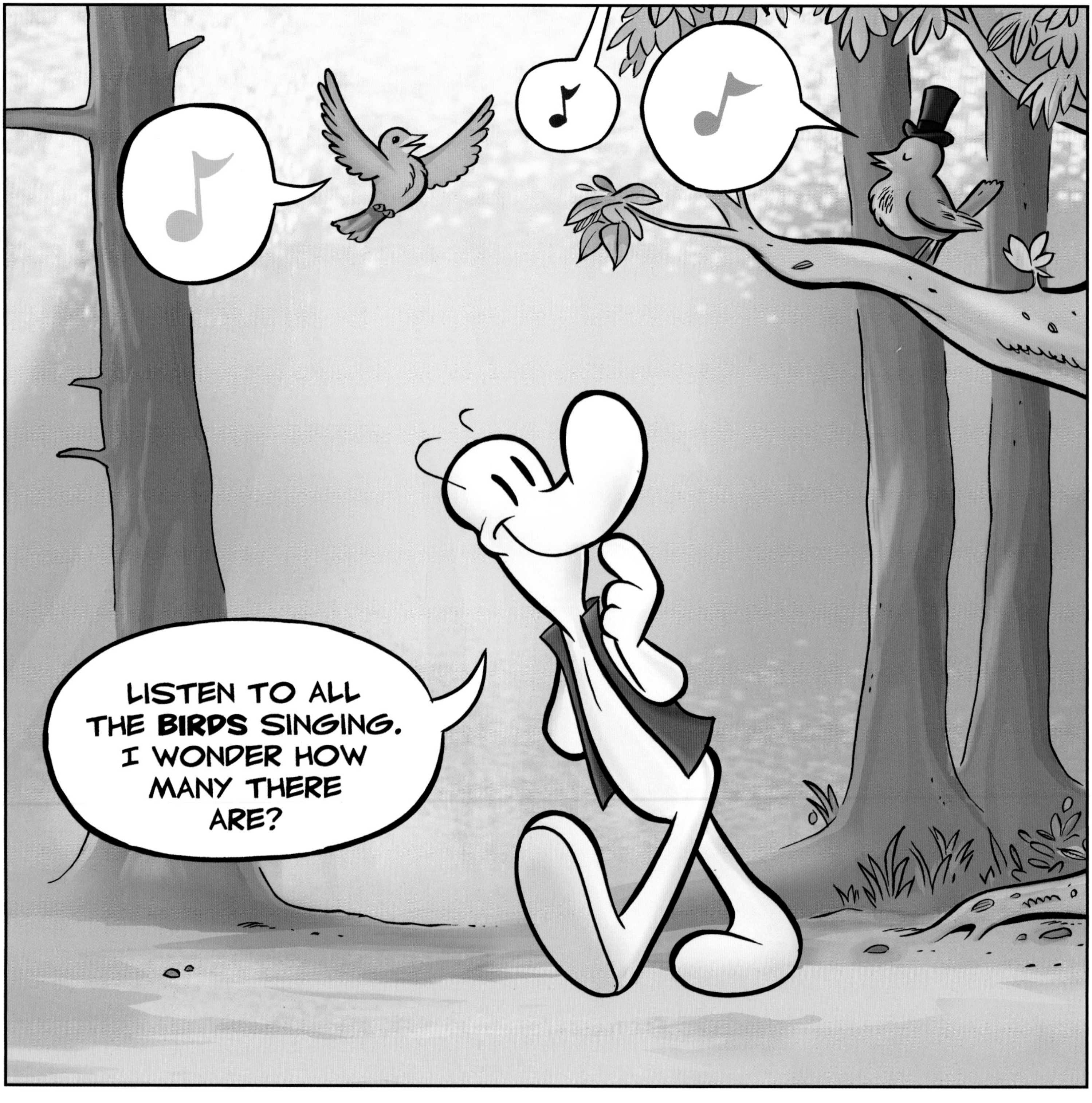
LISTEN TO ALL THE BIRDS SINGING. I WONDER HOW MANY THERE ARE?

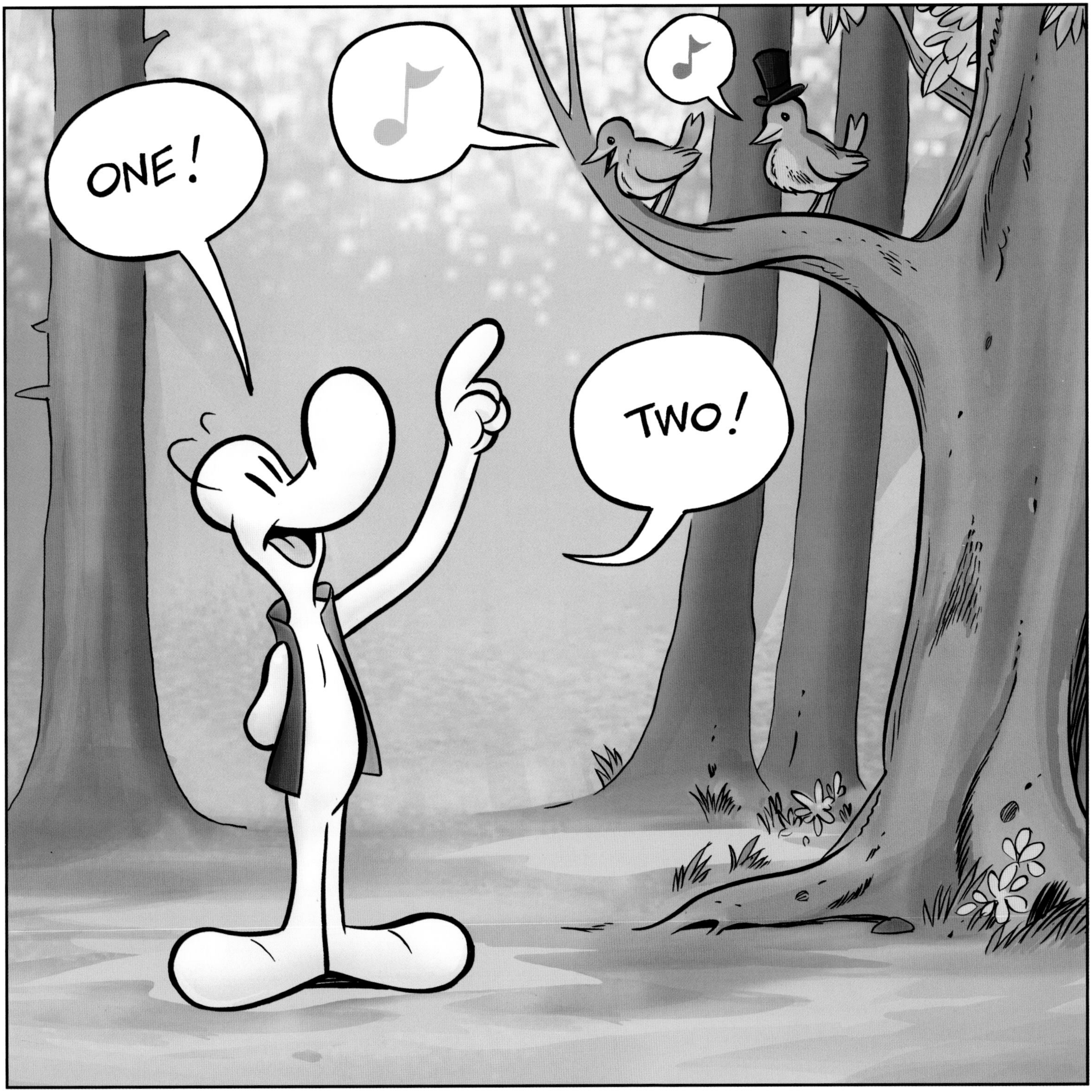
ONE!
TWO!

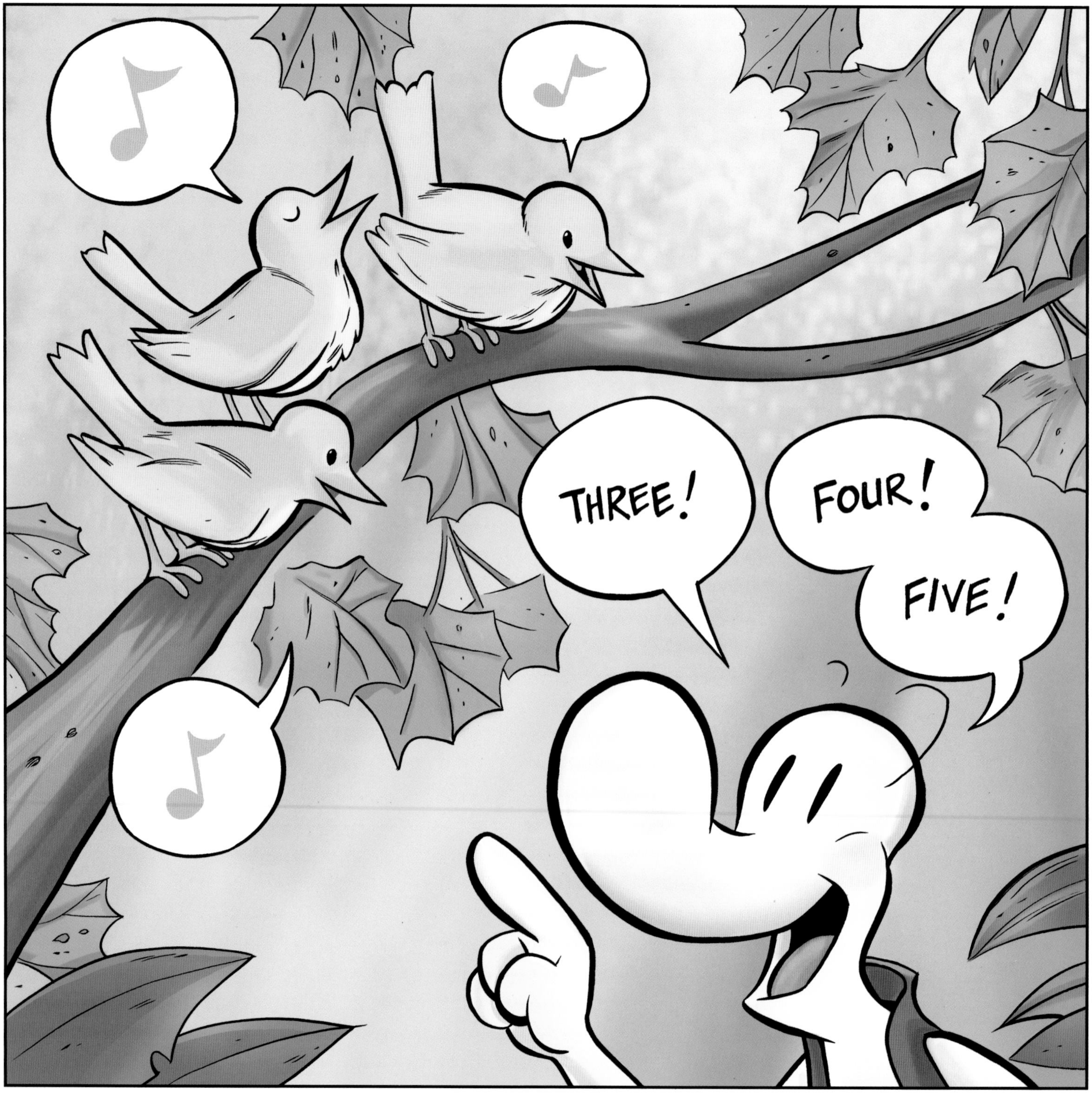
♪
♪
THREE!
FOUR!
FIVE!
♪

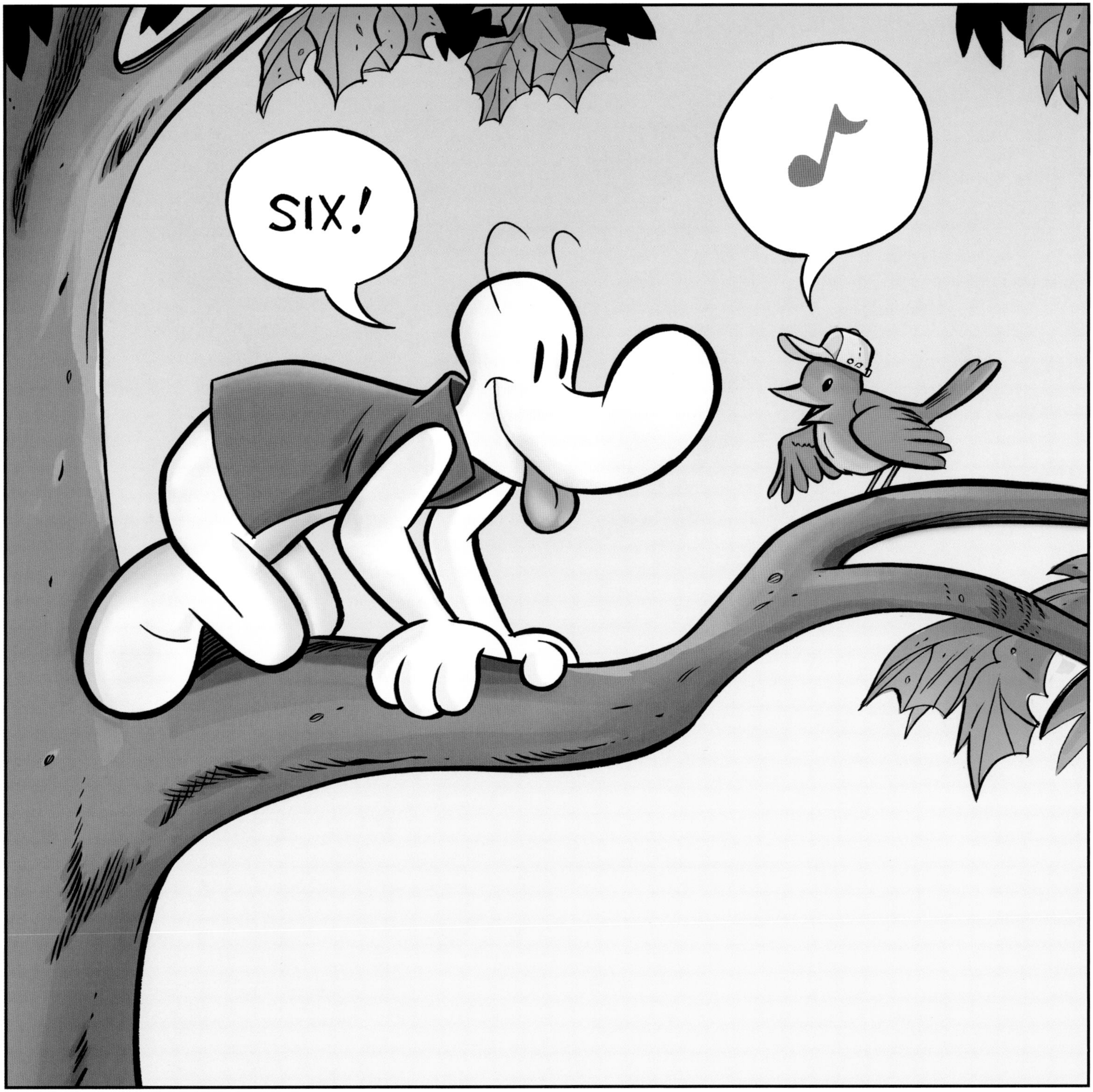
SIX!
♪

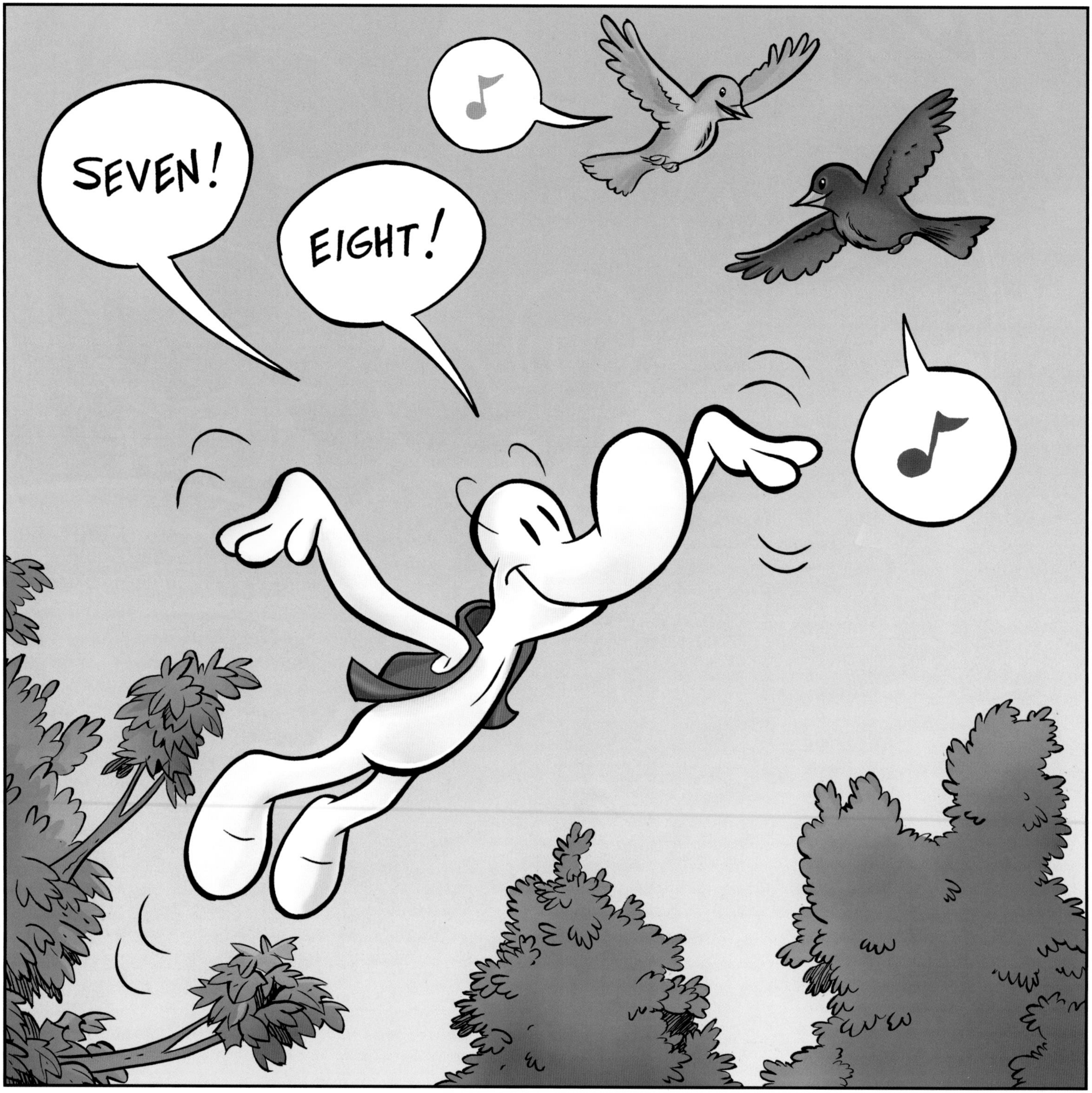
SEVEN!
EIGHT!

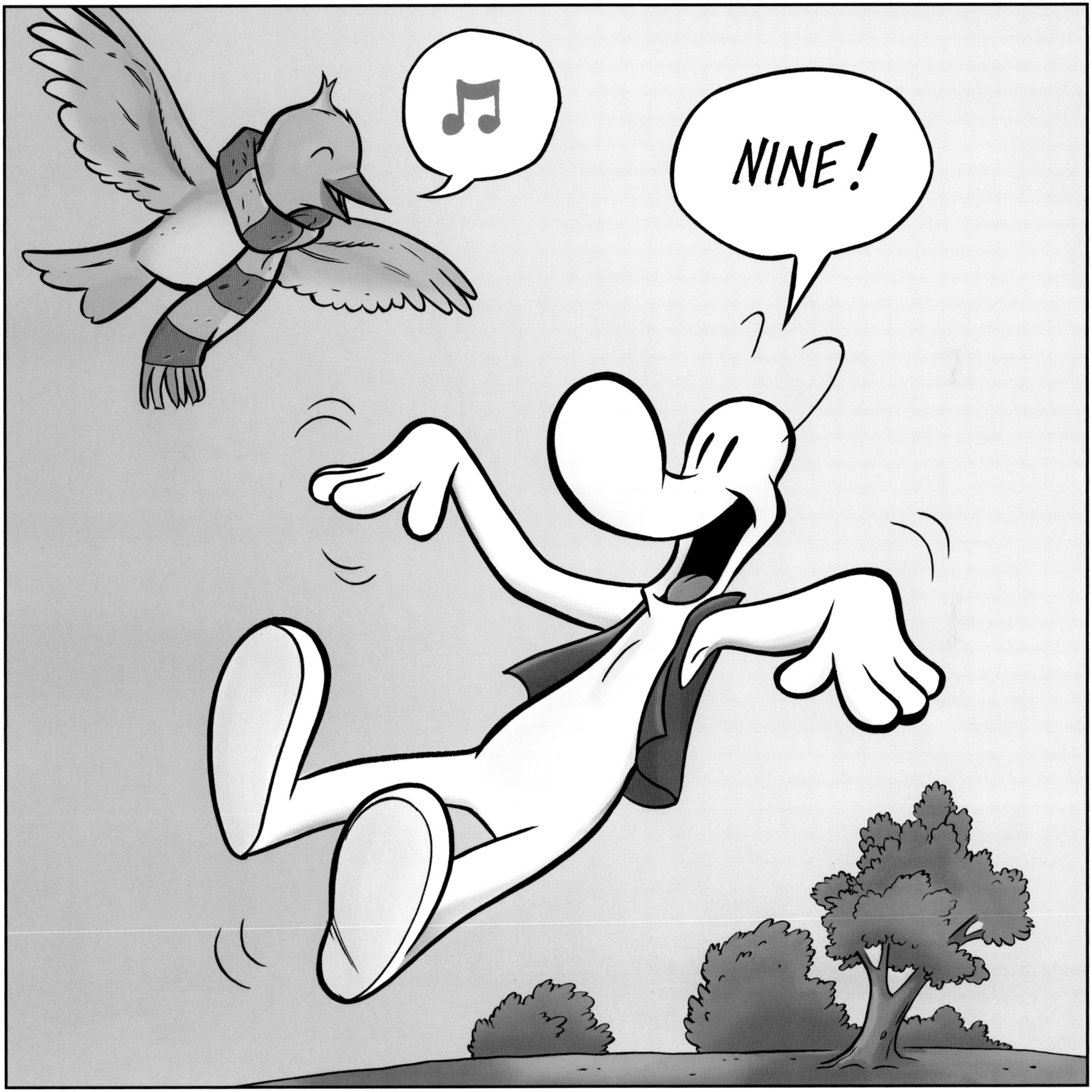
♫
NINE!

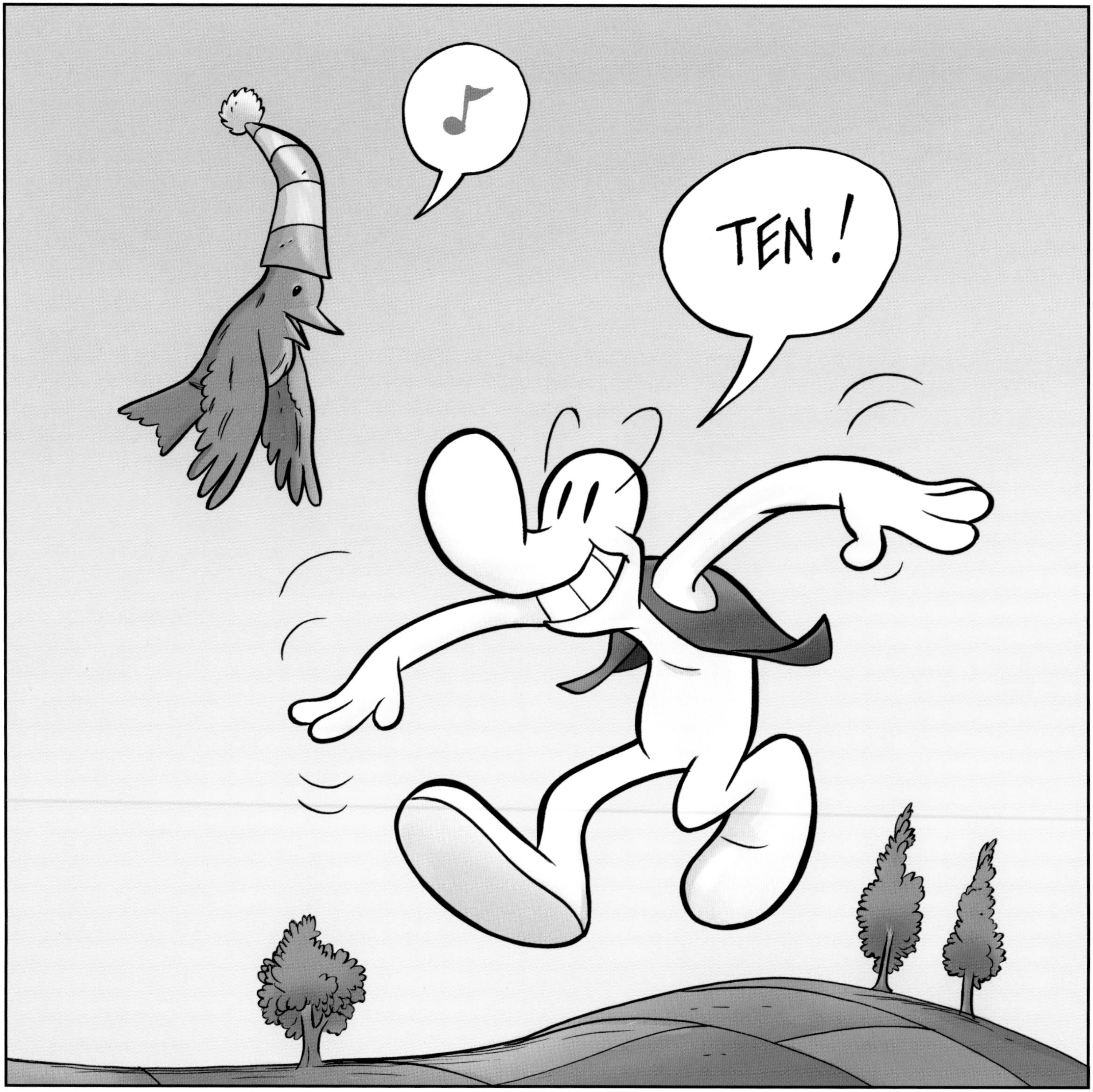
♪
TEN!

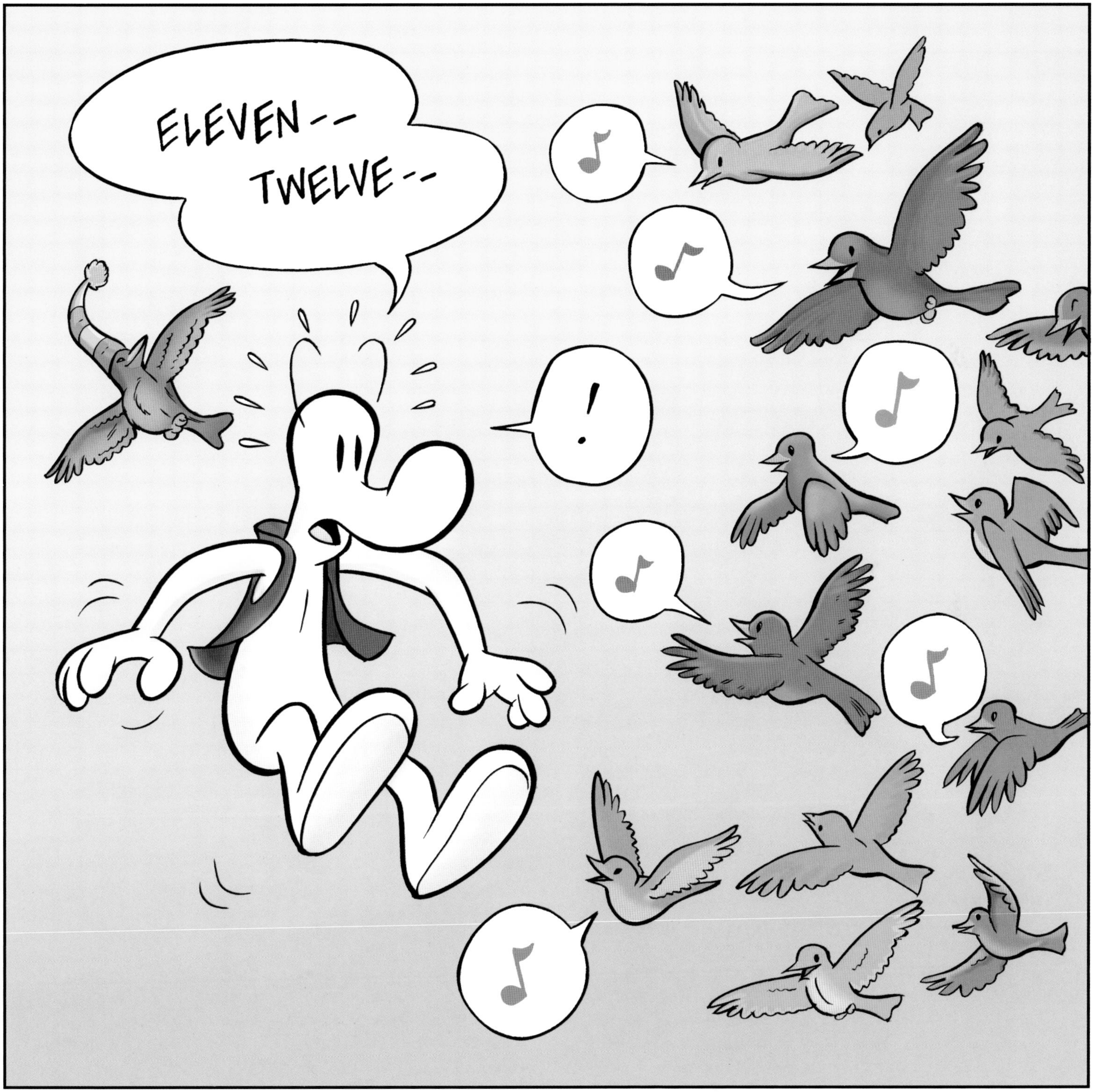
ELEVEN--
TWELVE--
!

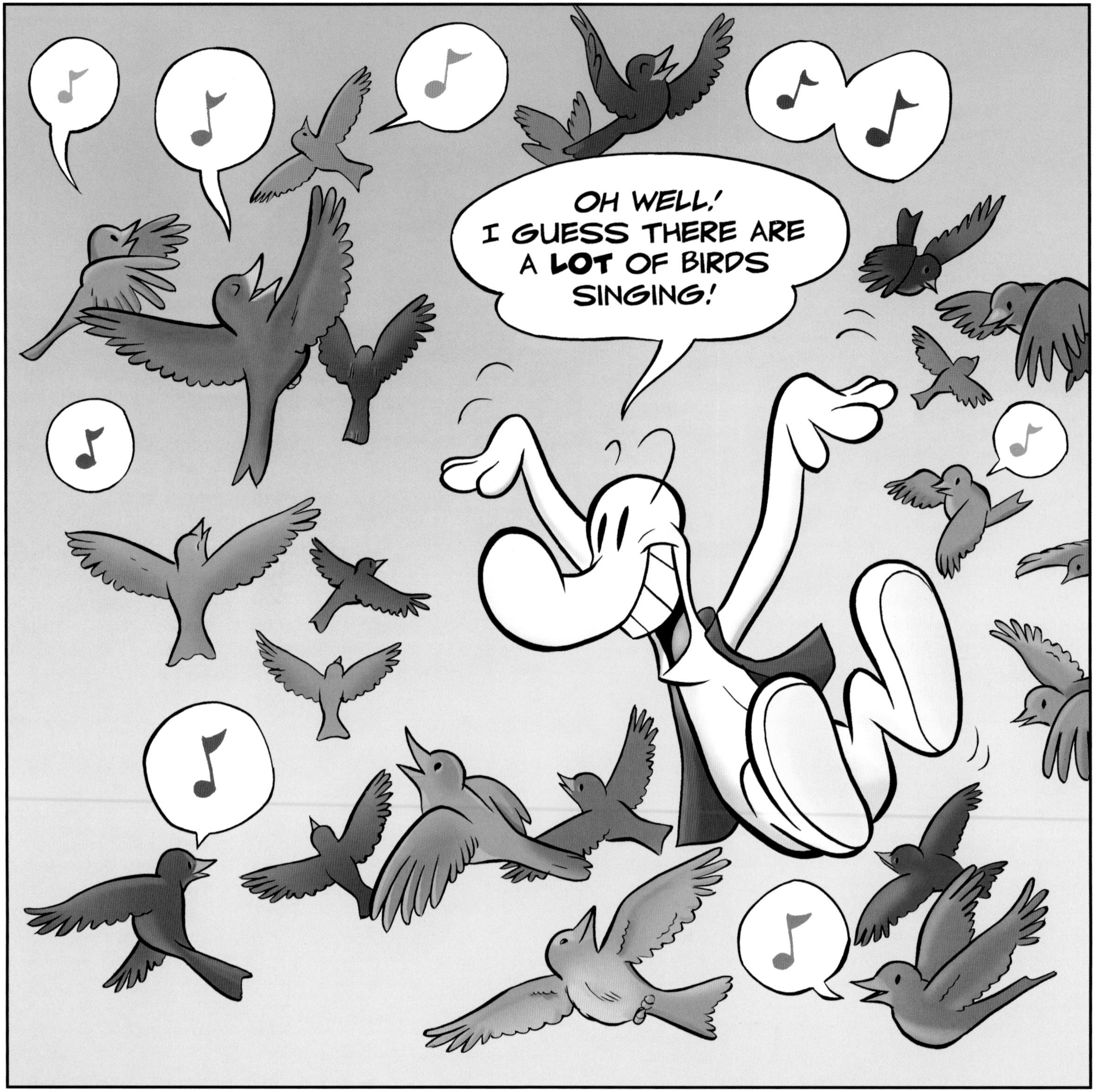
OH WELL! I GUESS THERE ARE A **LOT** OF BIRDS SINGING!

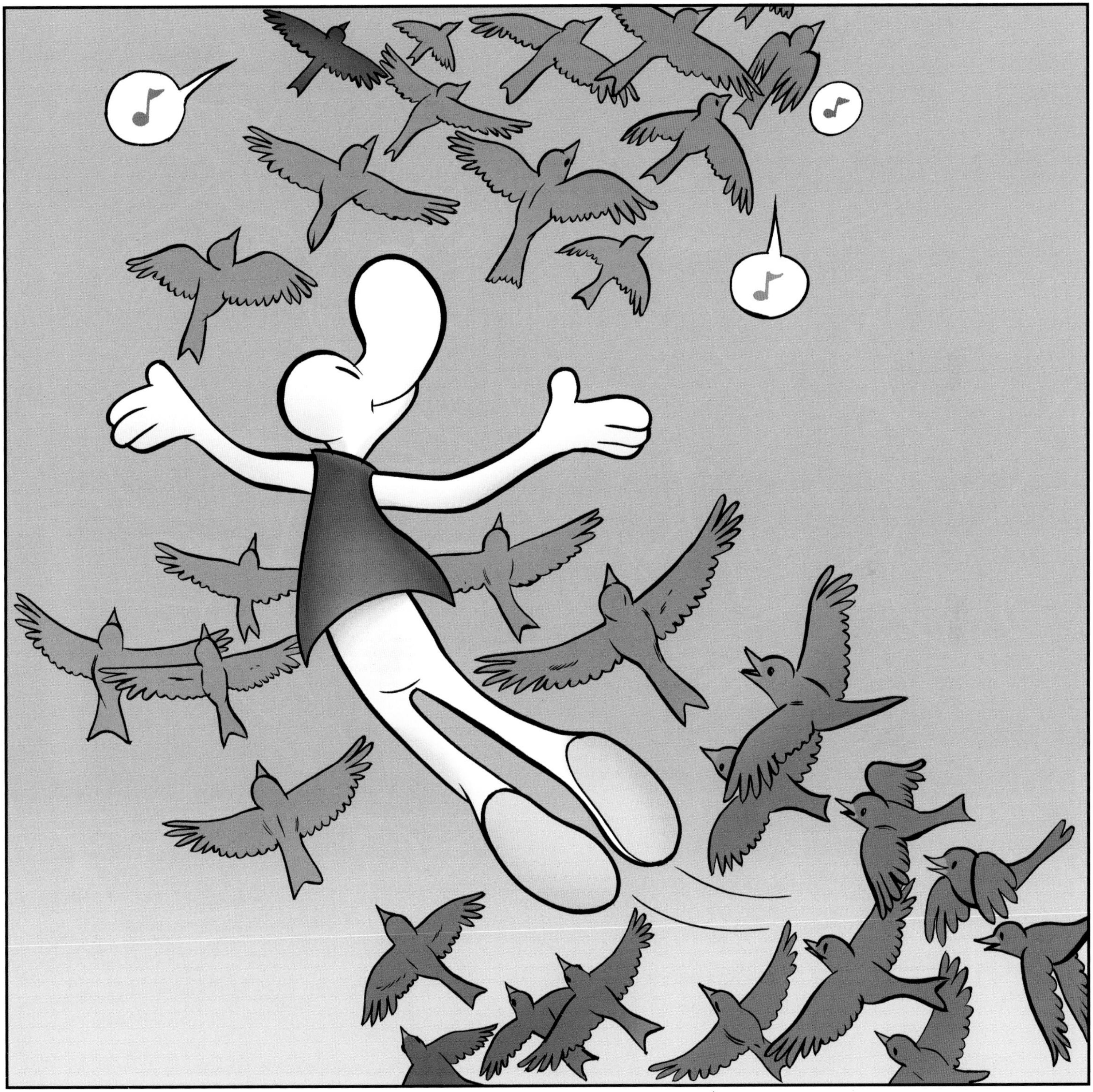

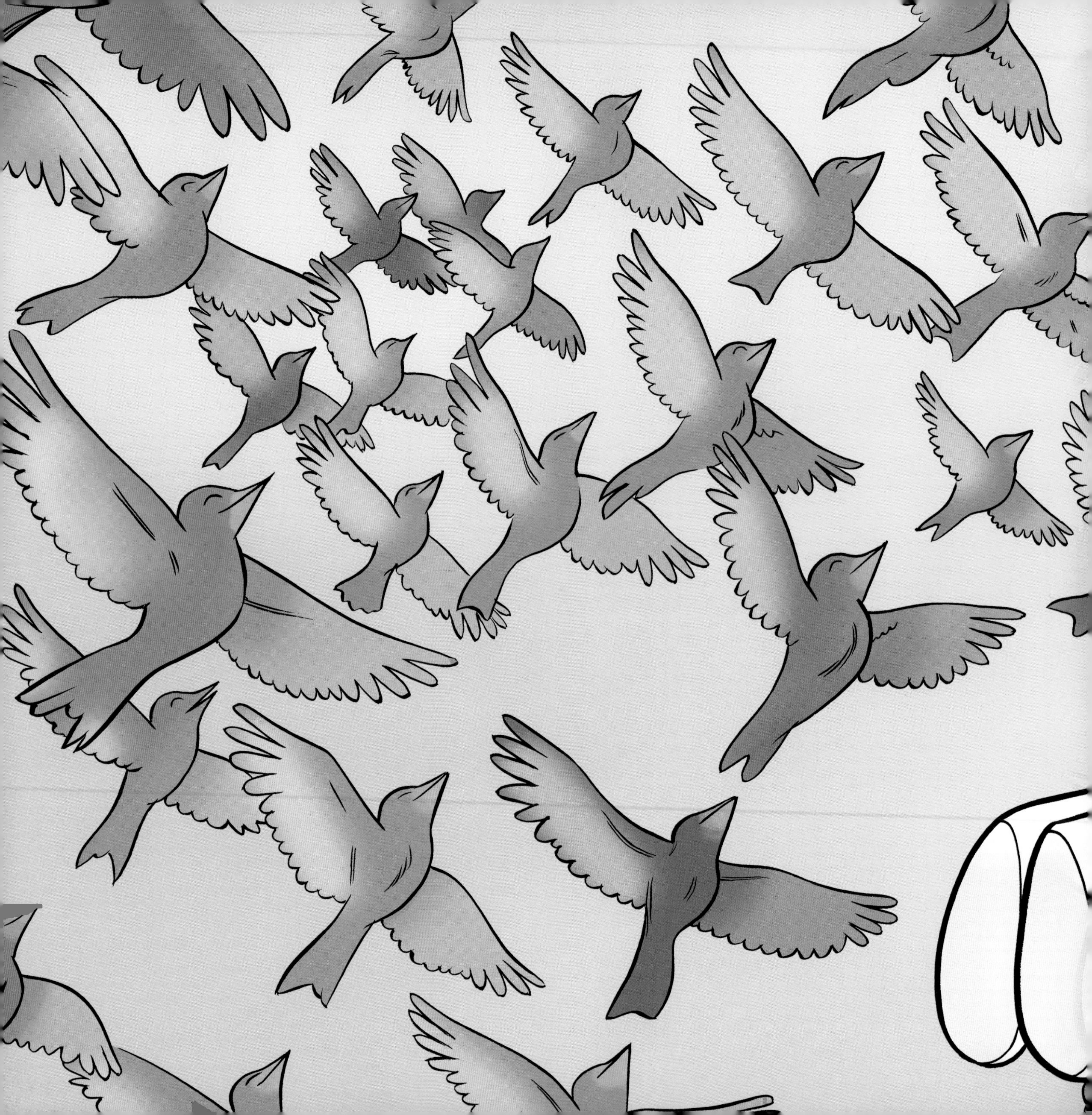

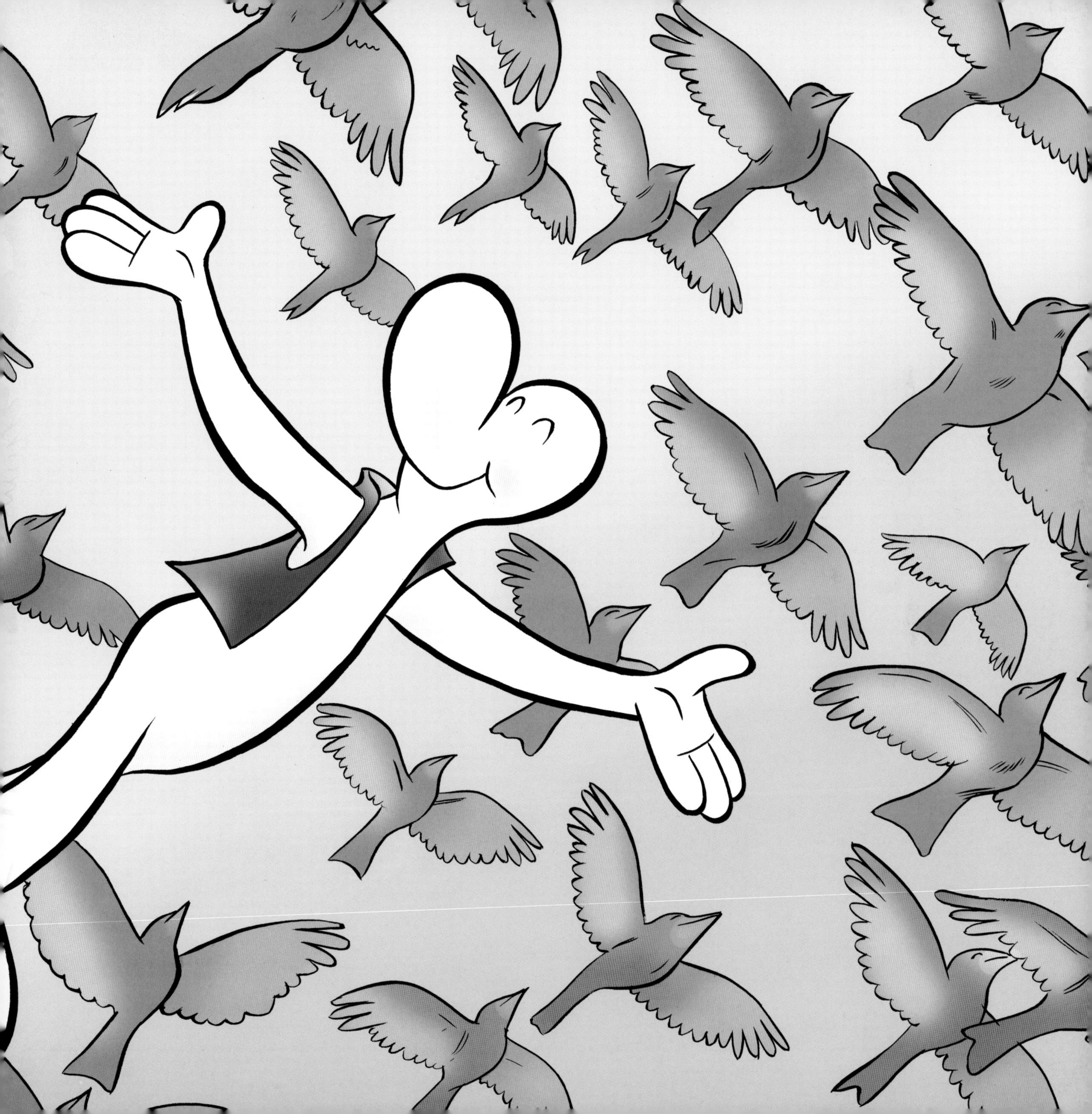

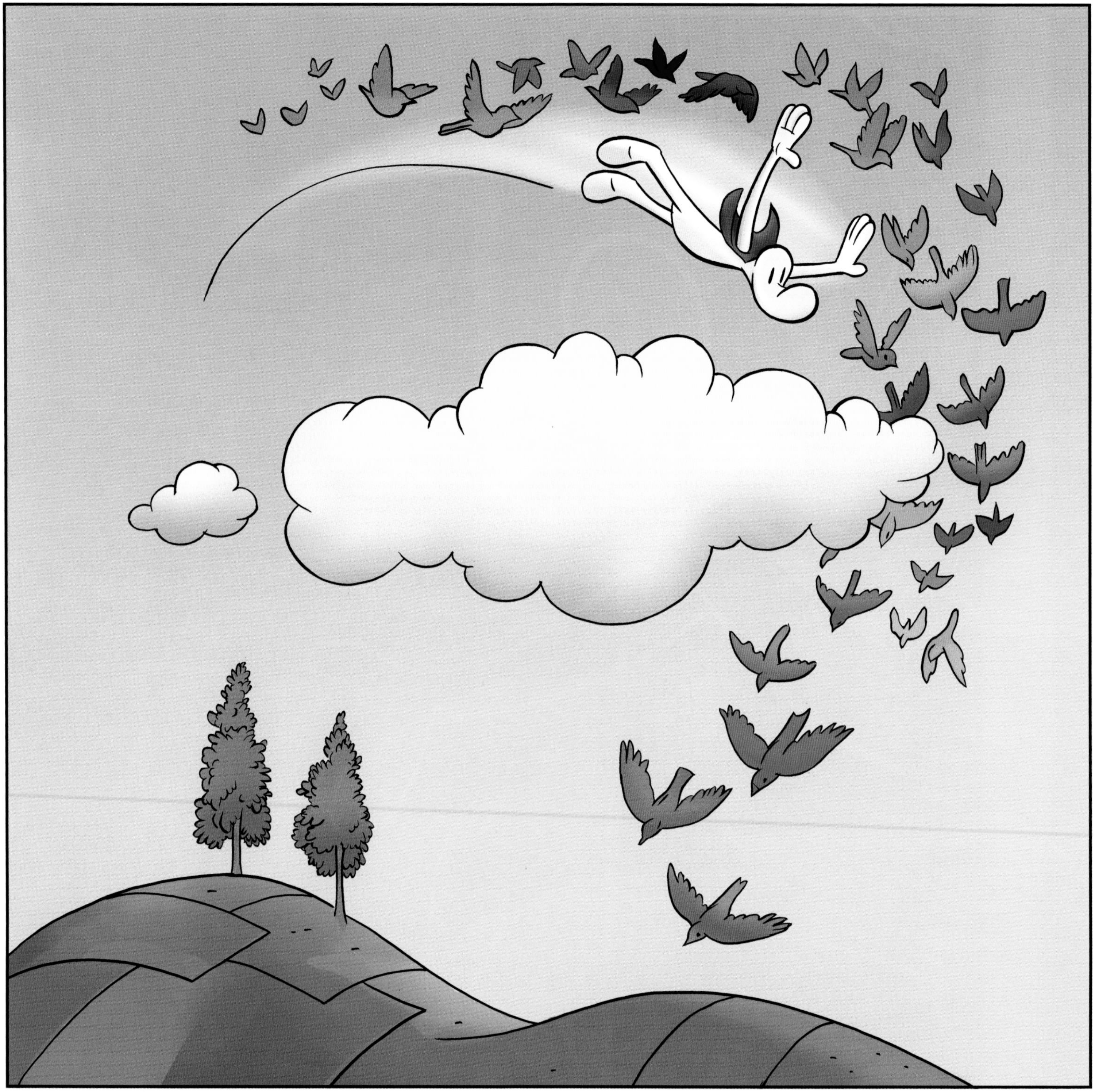

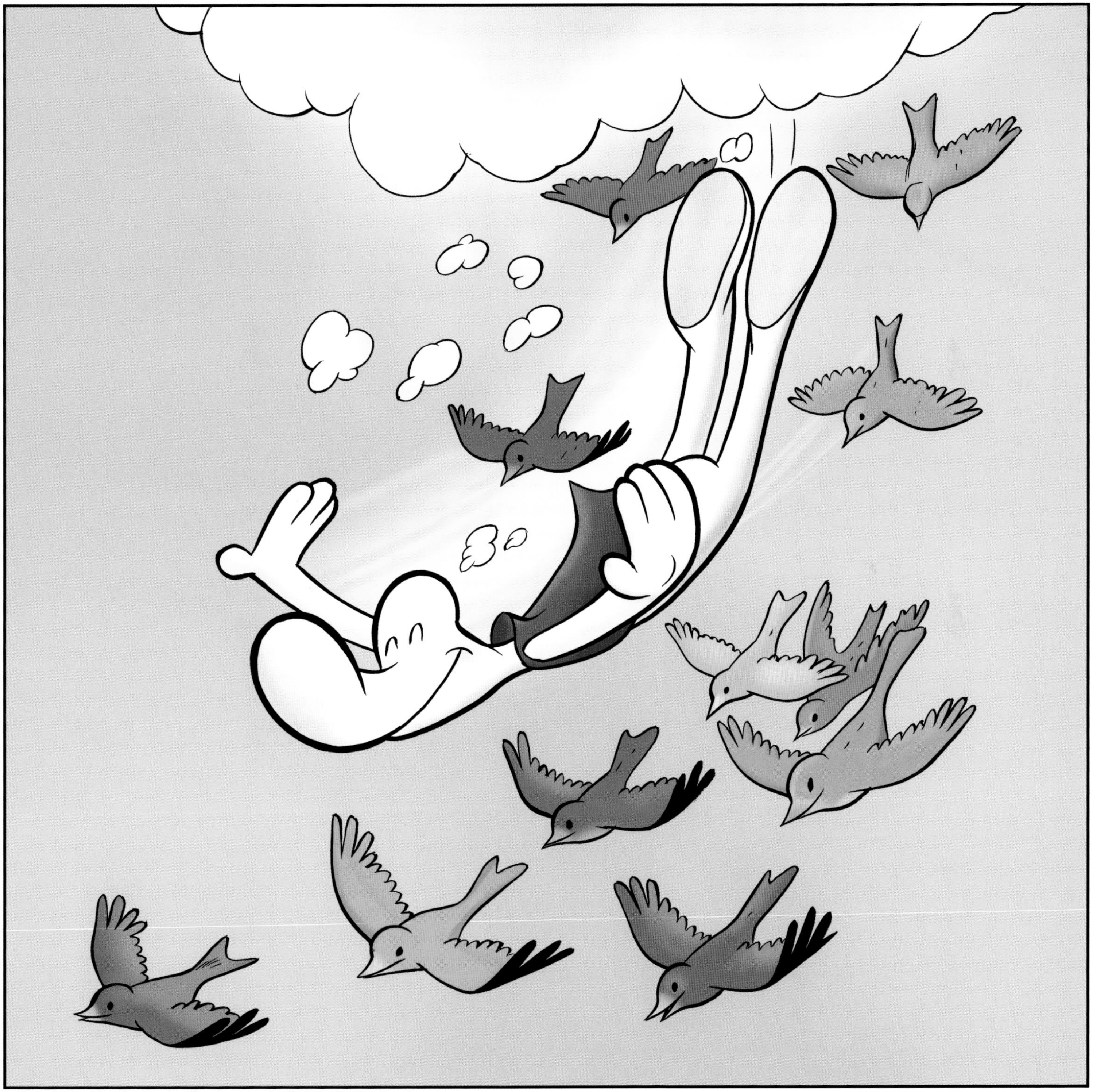

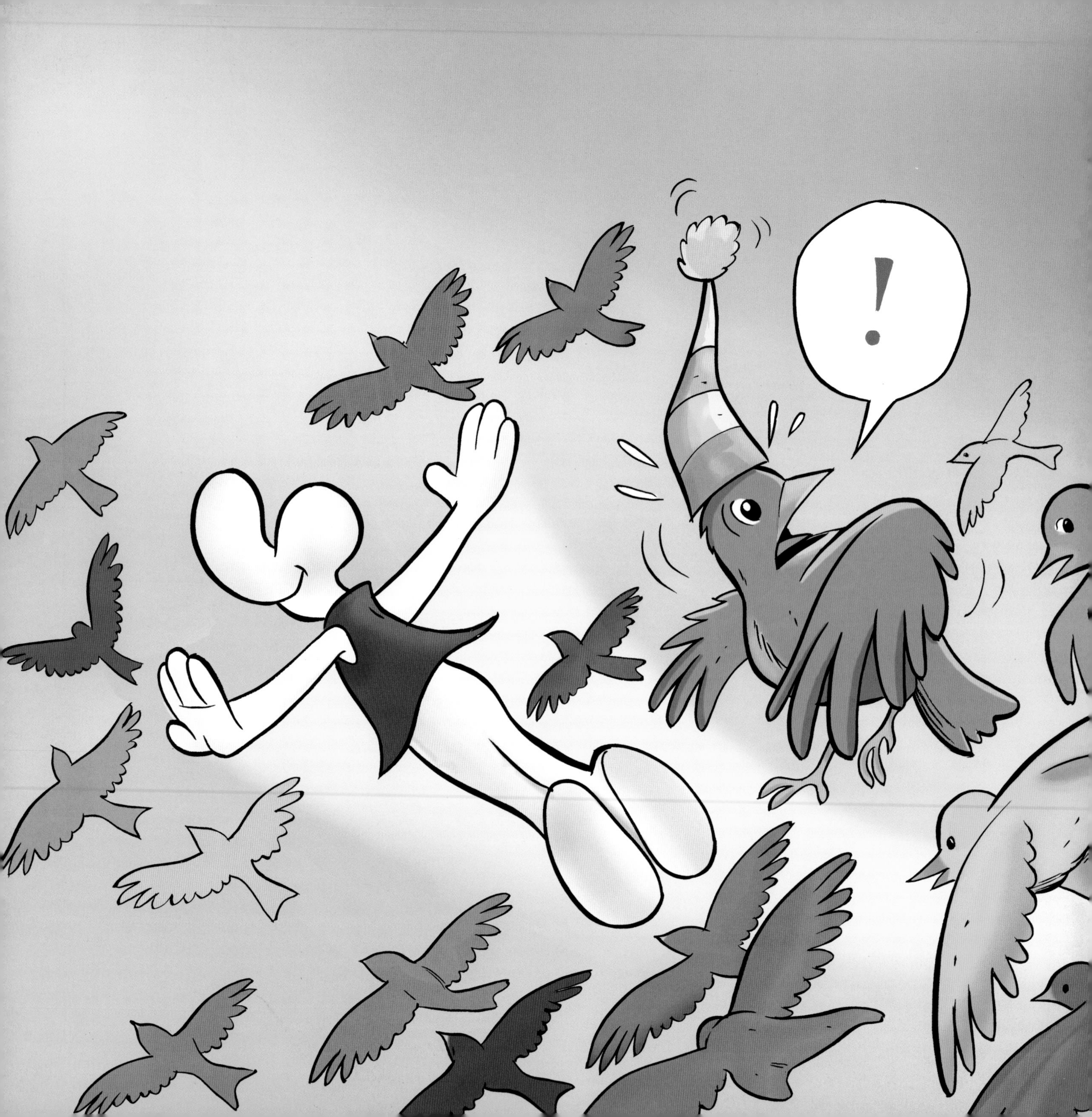
!

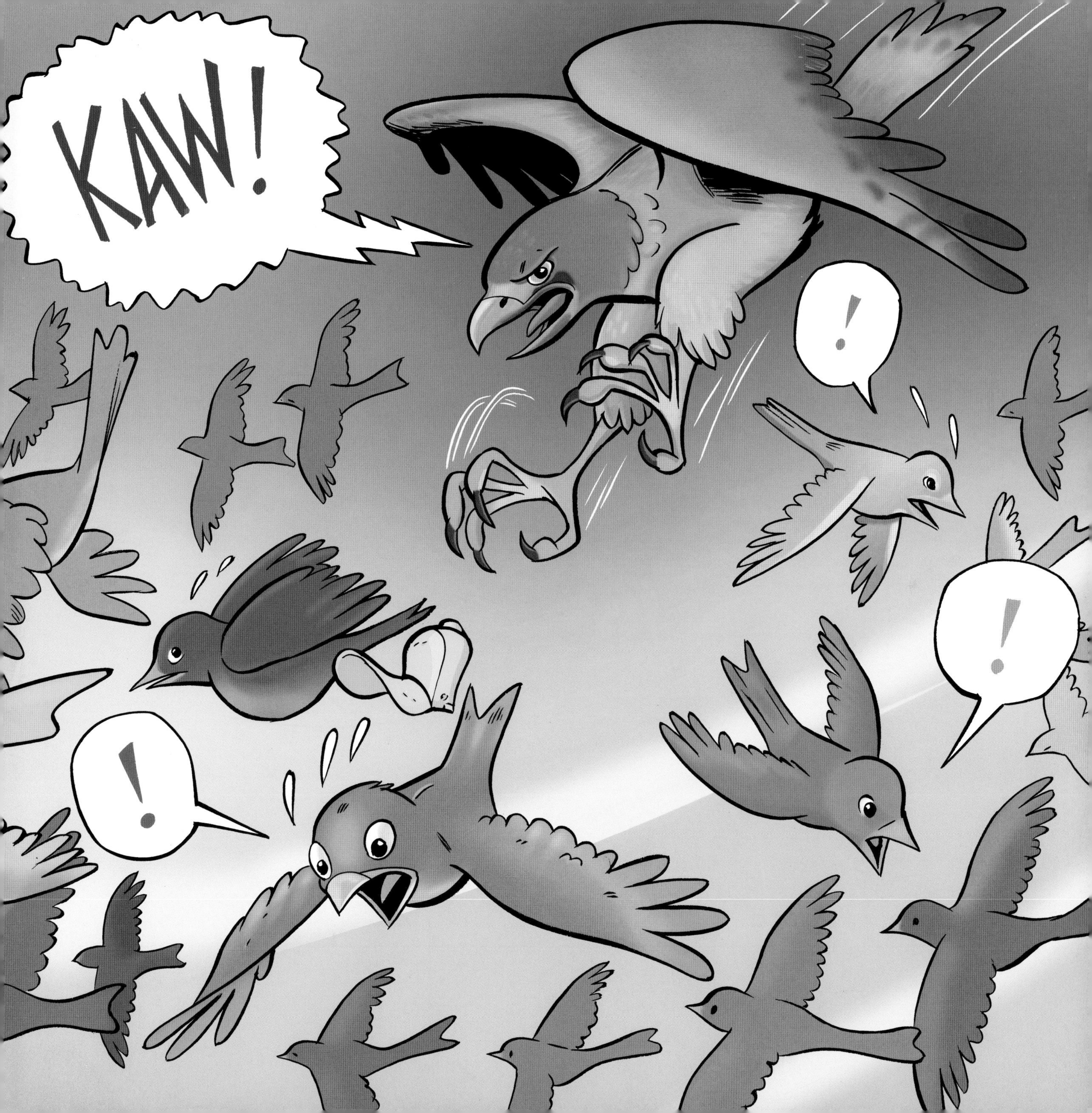
KAW!
!
!
!

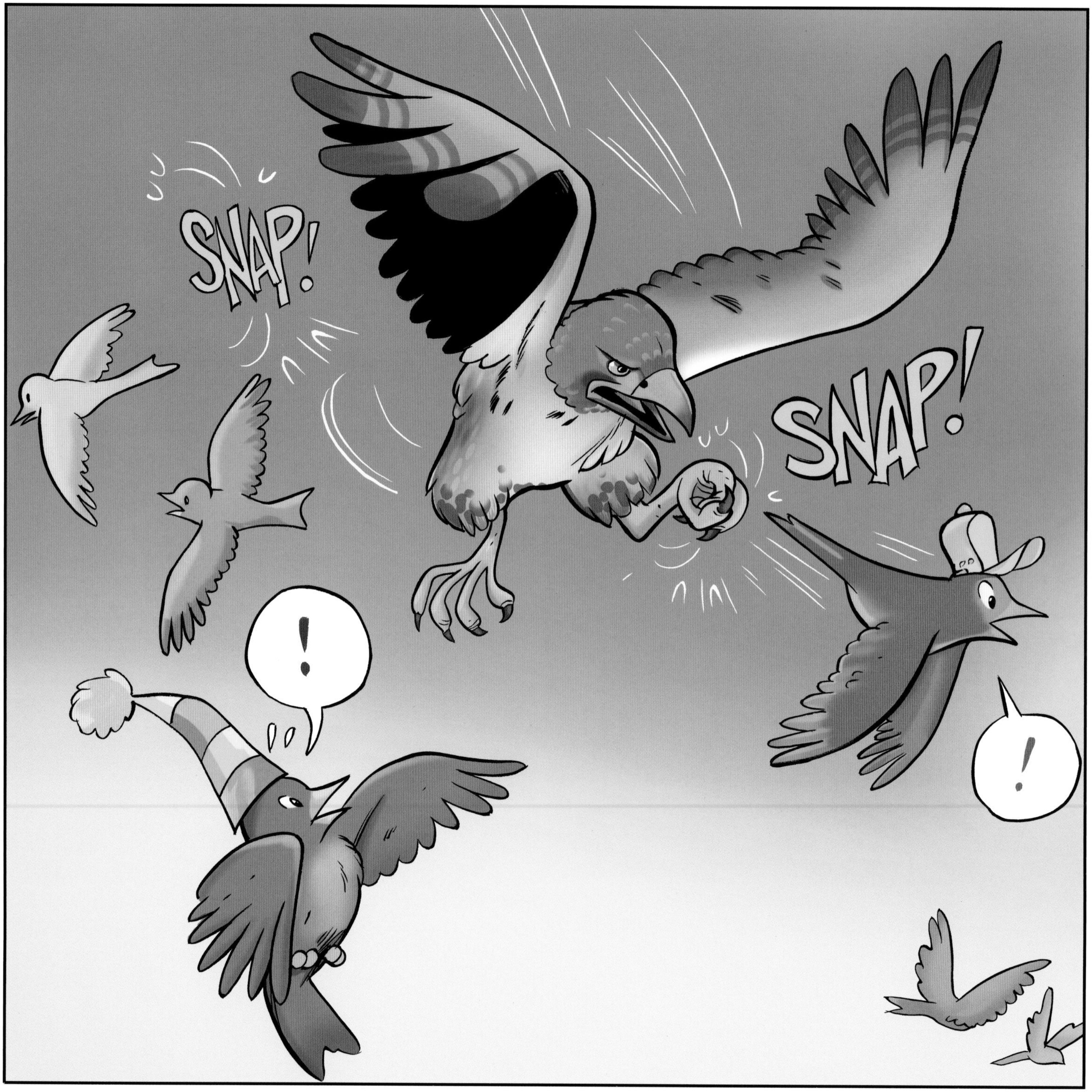
SNAP!
SNAP!
!
!

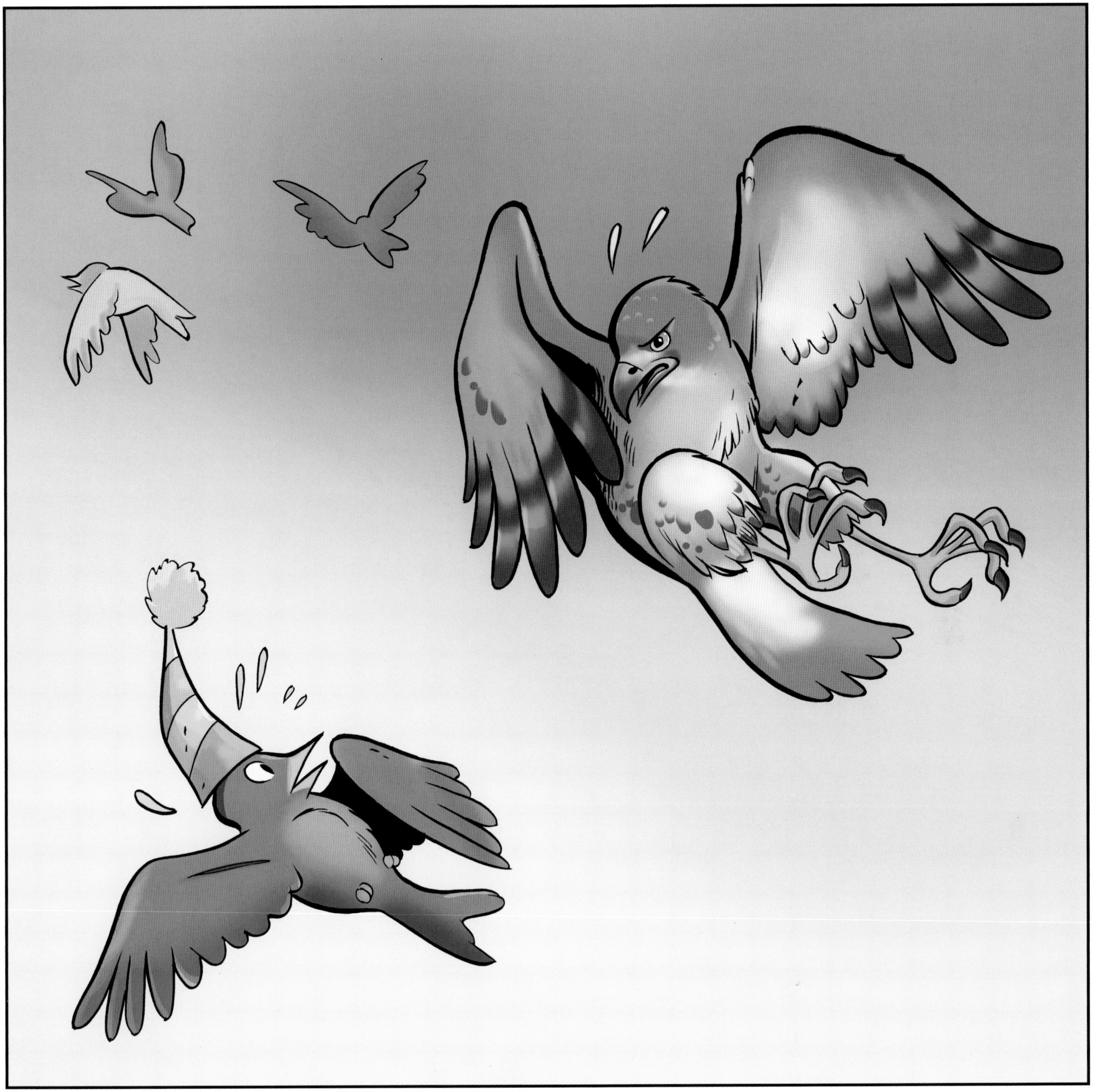

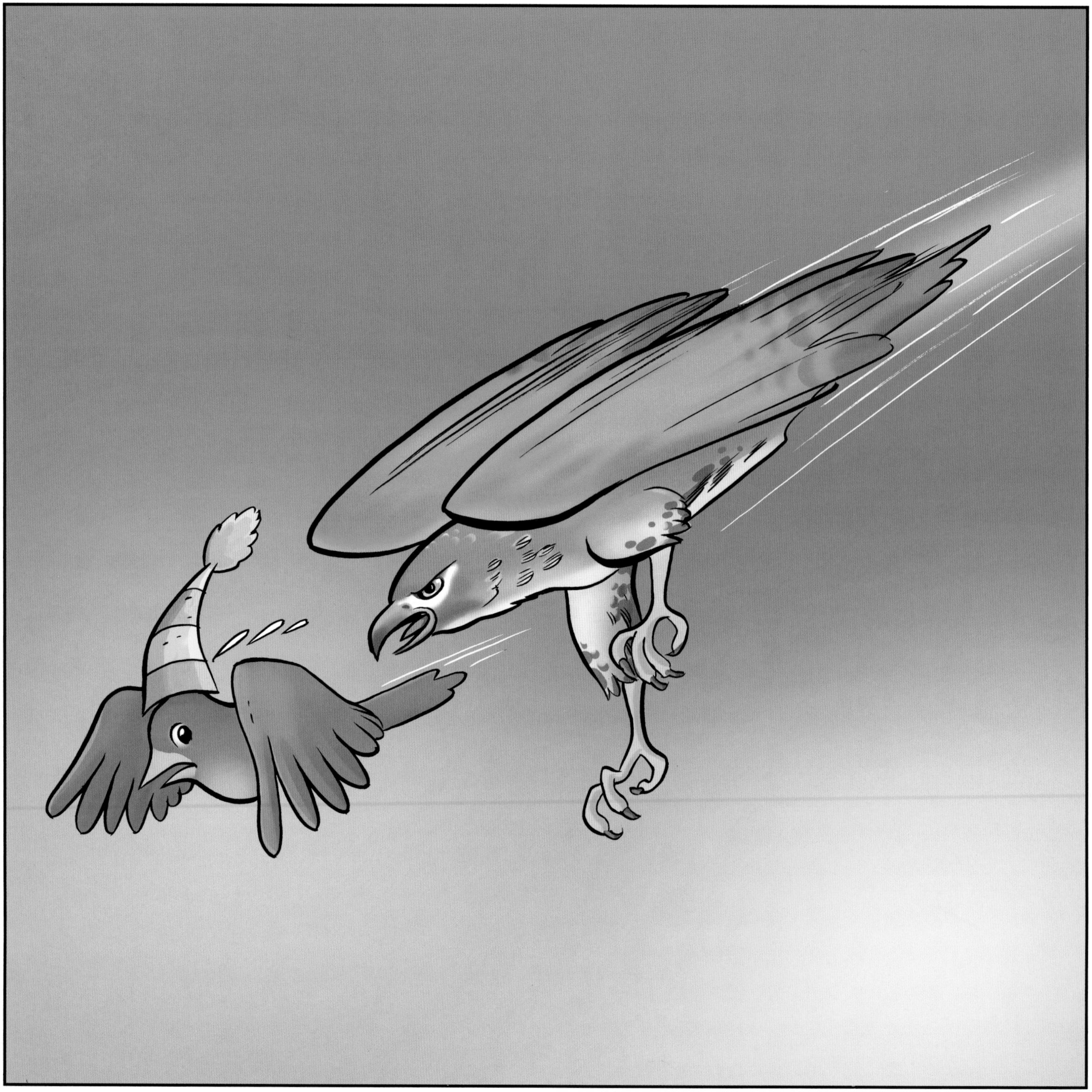

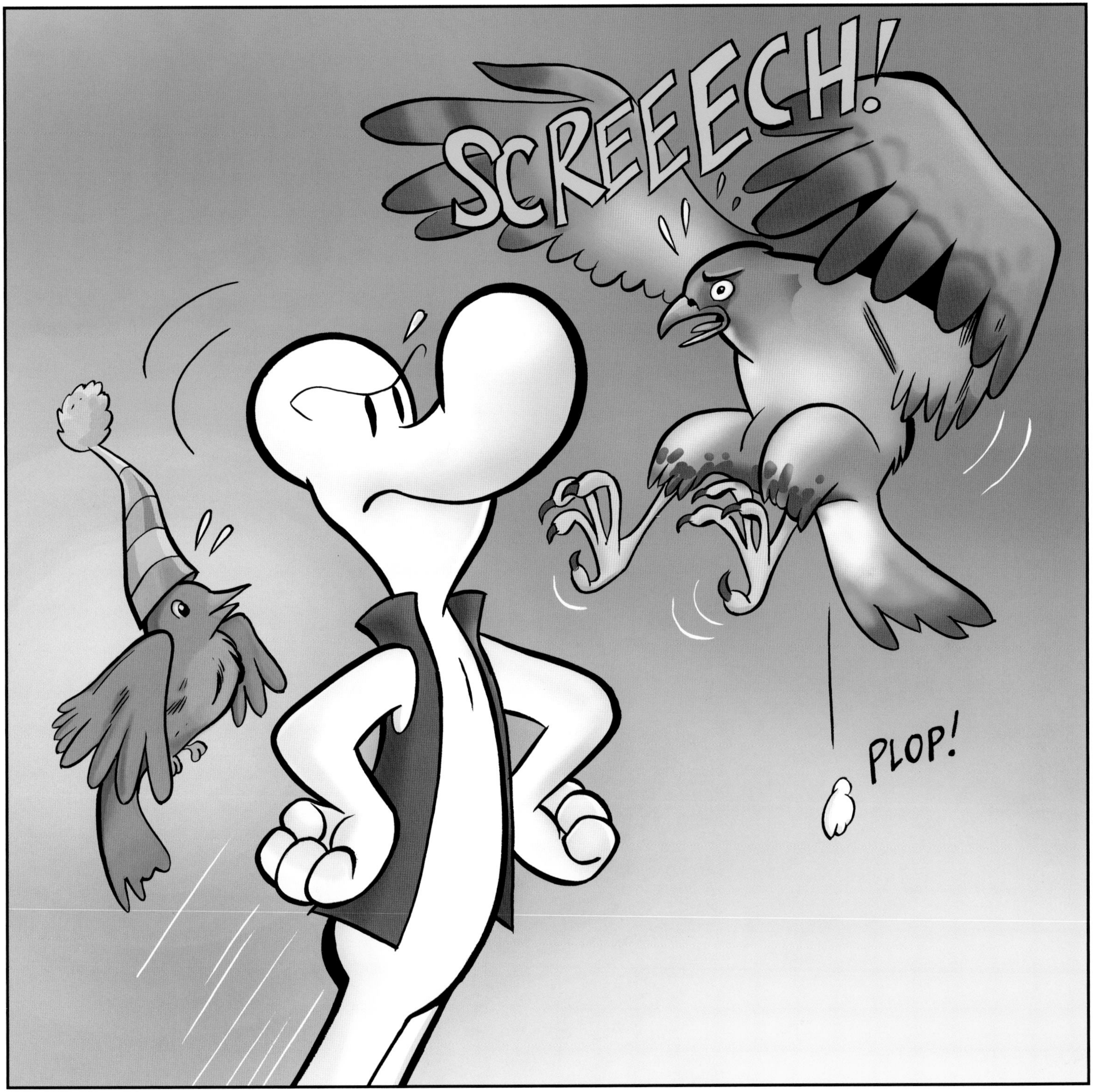
SCREEECH!
PLOP!

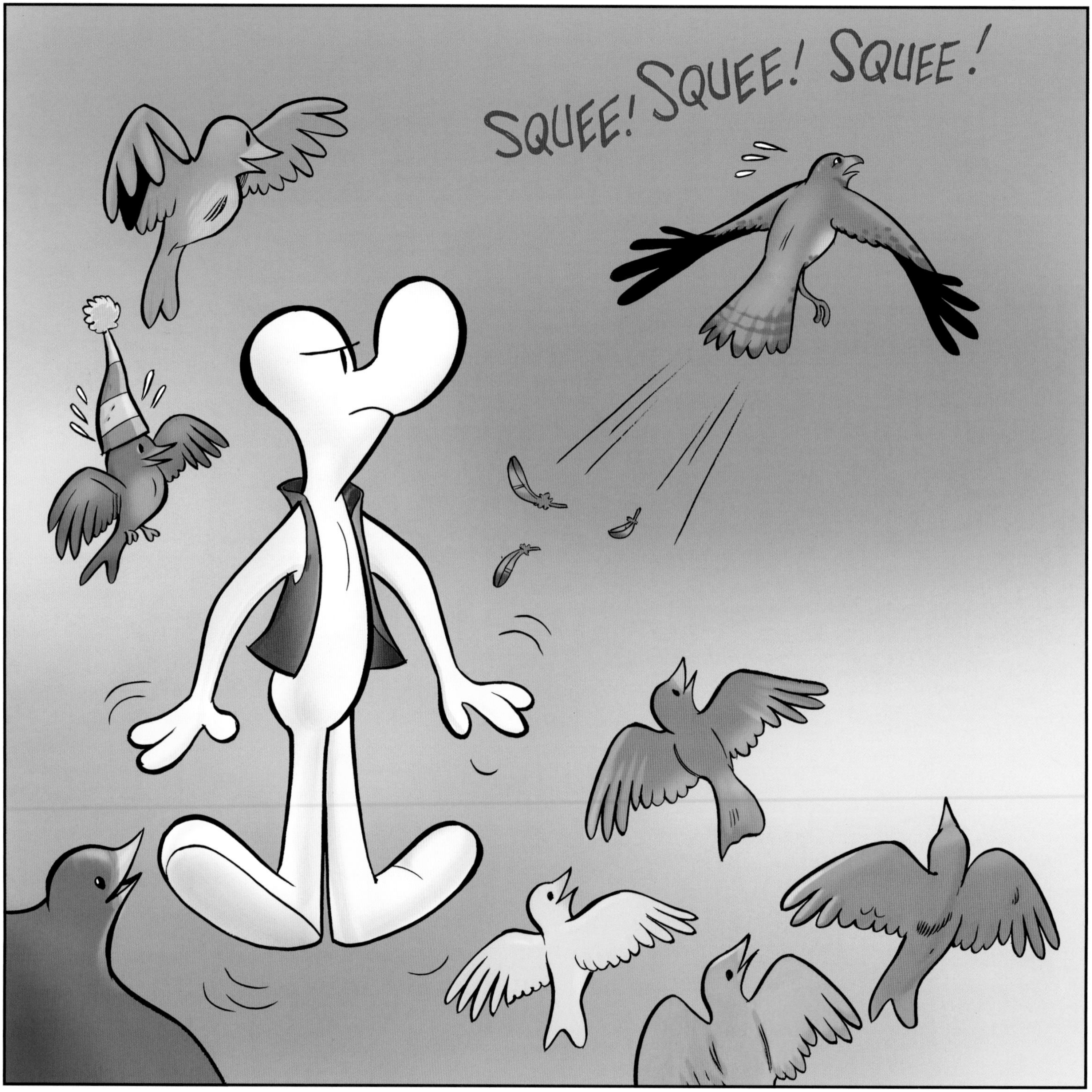
SQUEE! SQUEE! SQUEE!

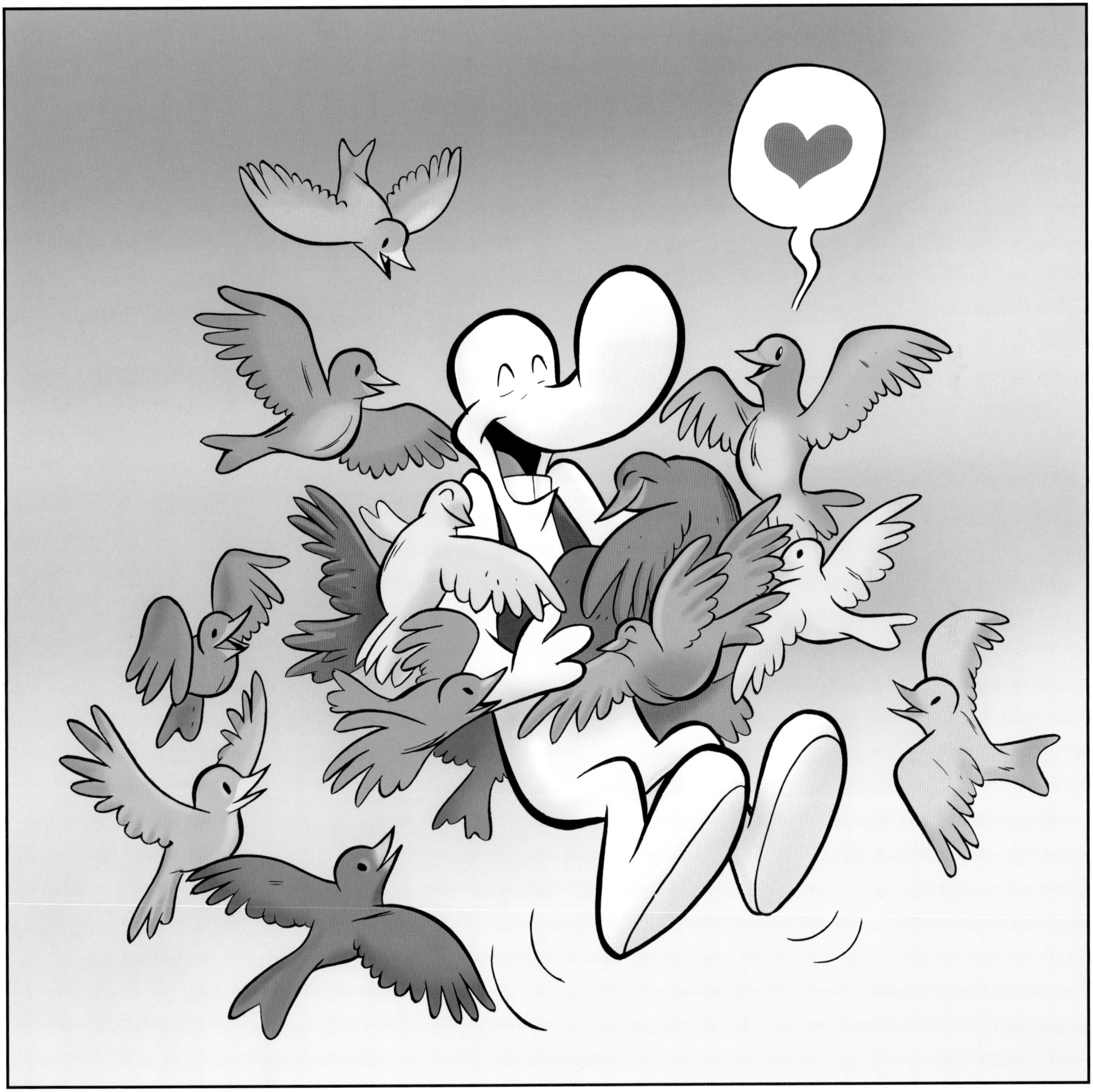

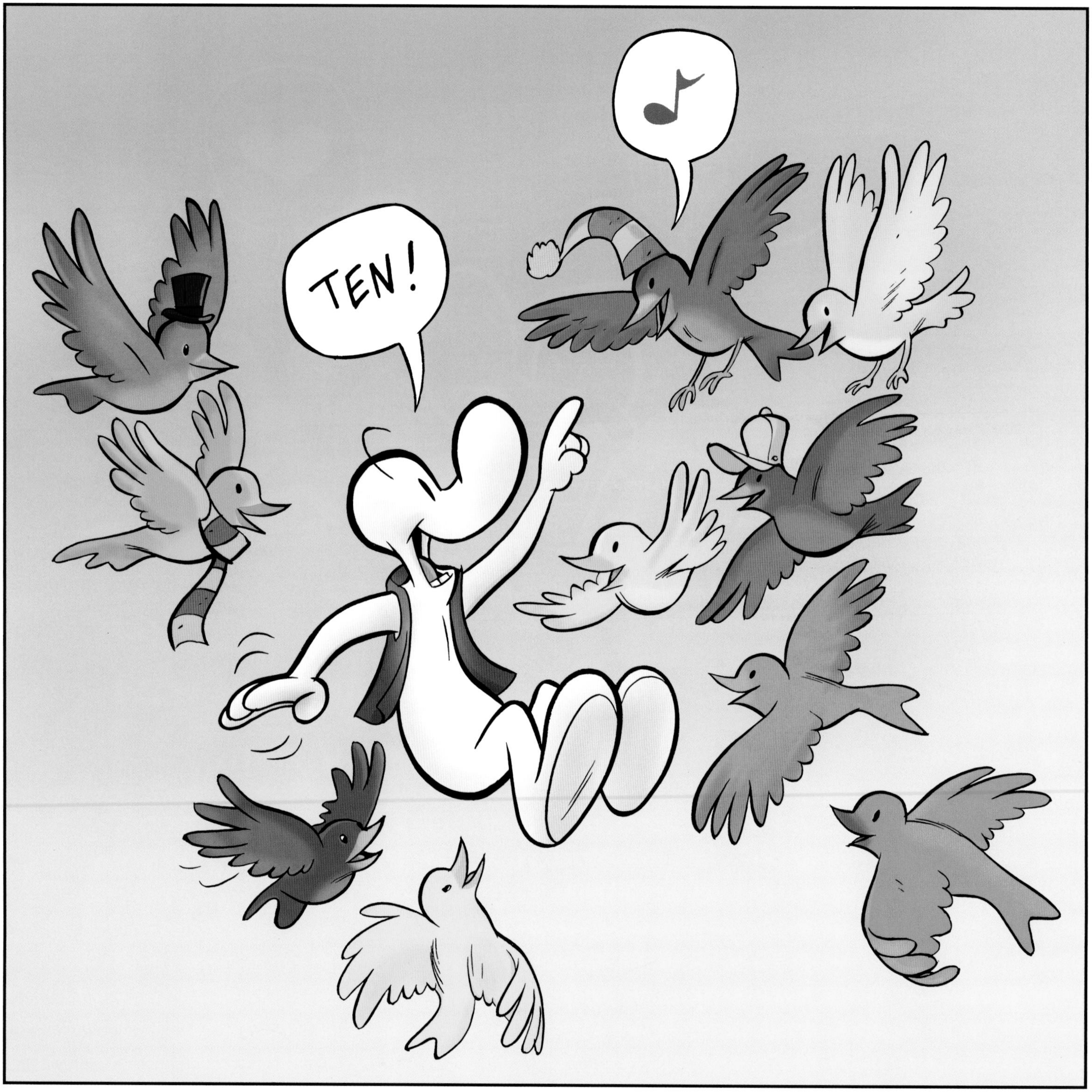
TEN!

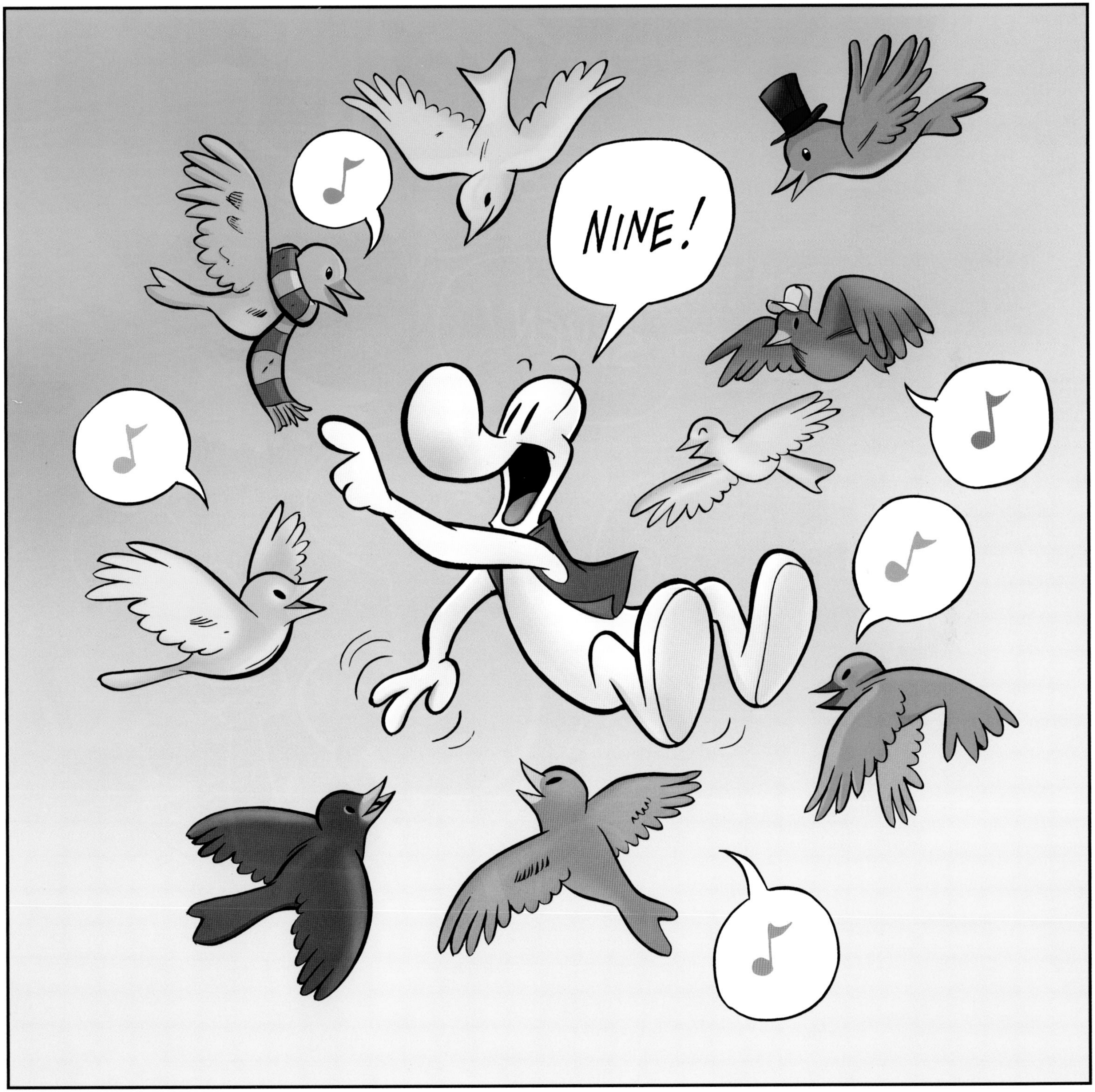
NINE!

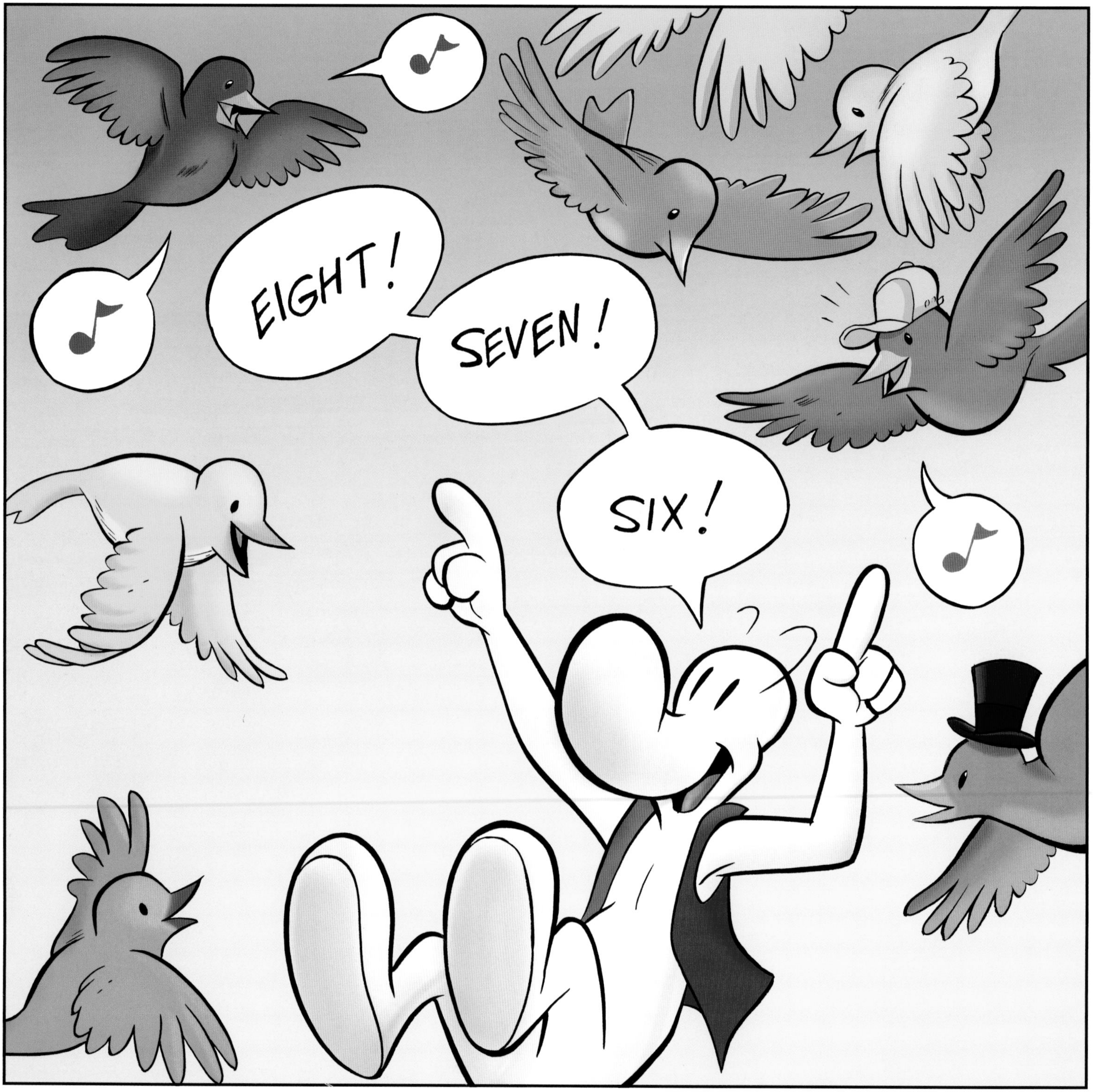
EIGHT!
SEVEN!
SIX!

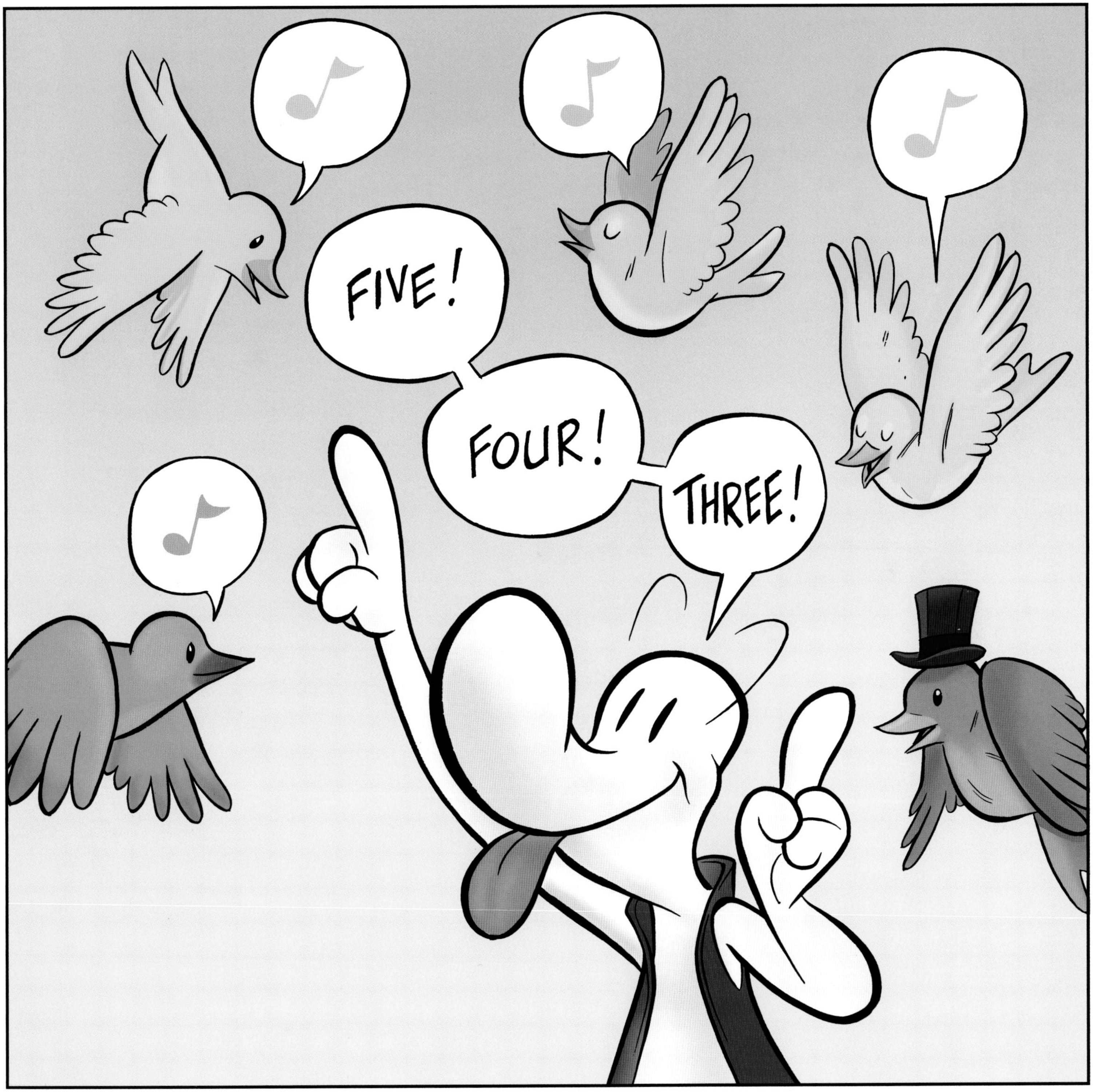
FIVE!
FOUR!
THREE!

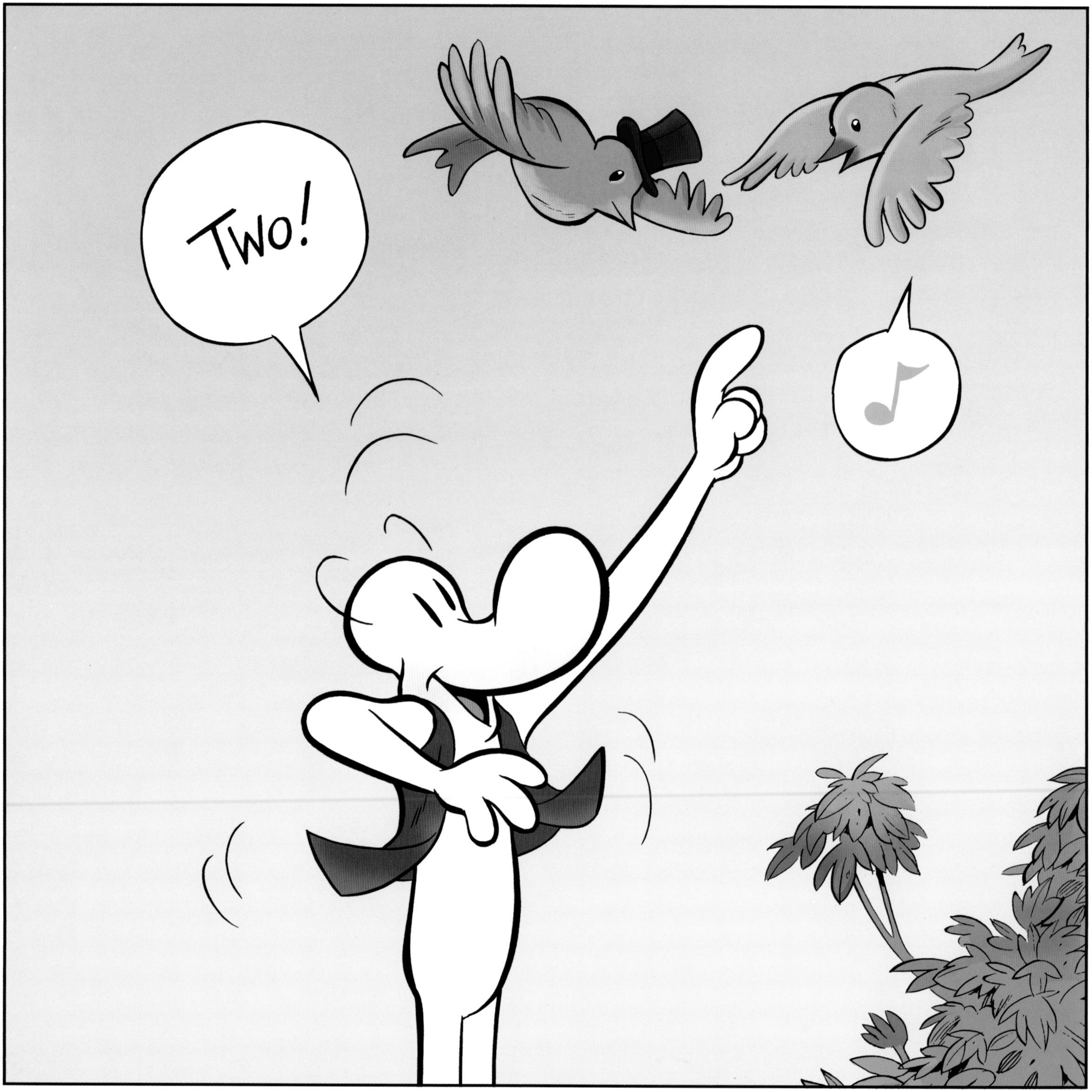
TWO!
♪

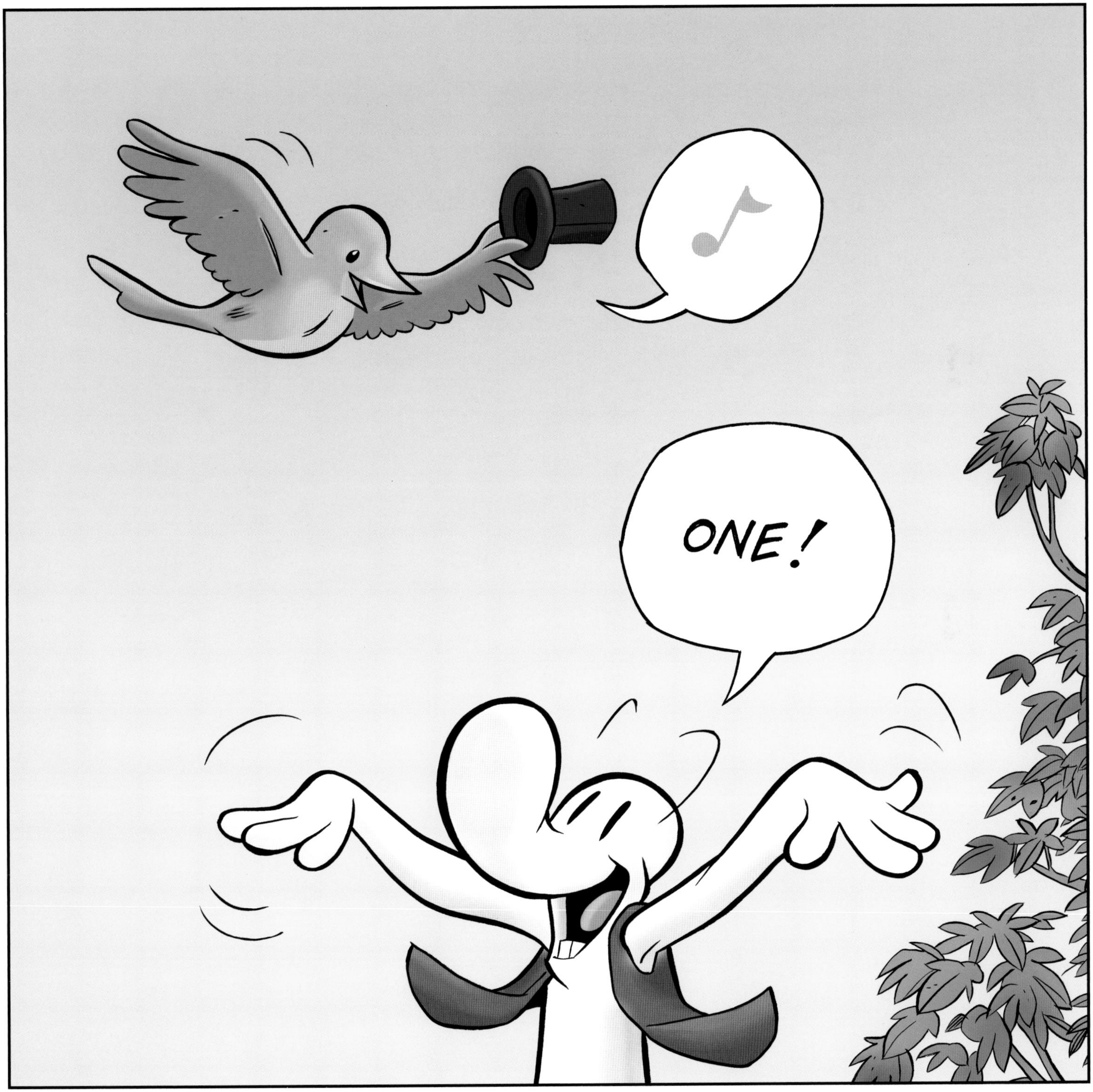
♪
ONE!

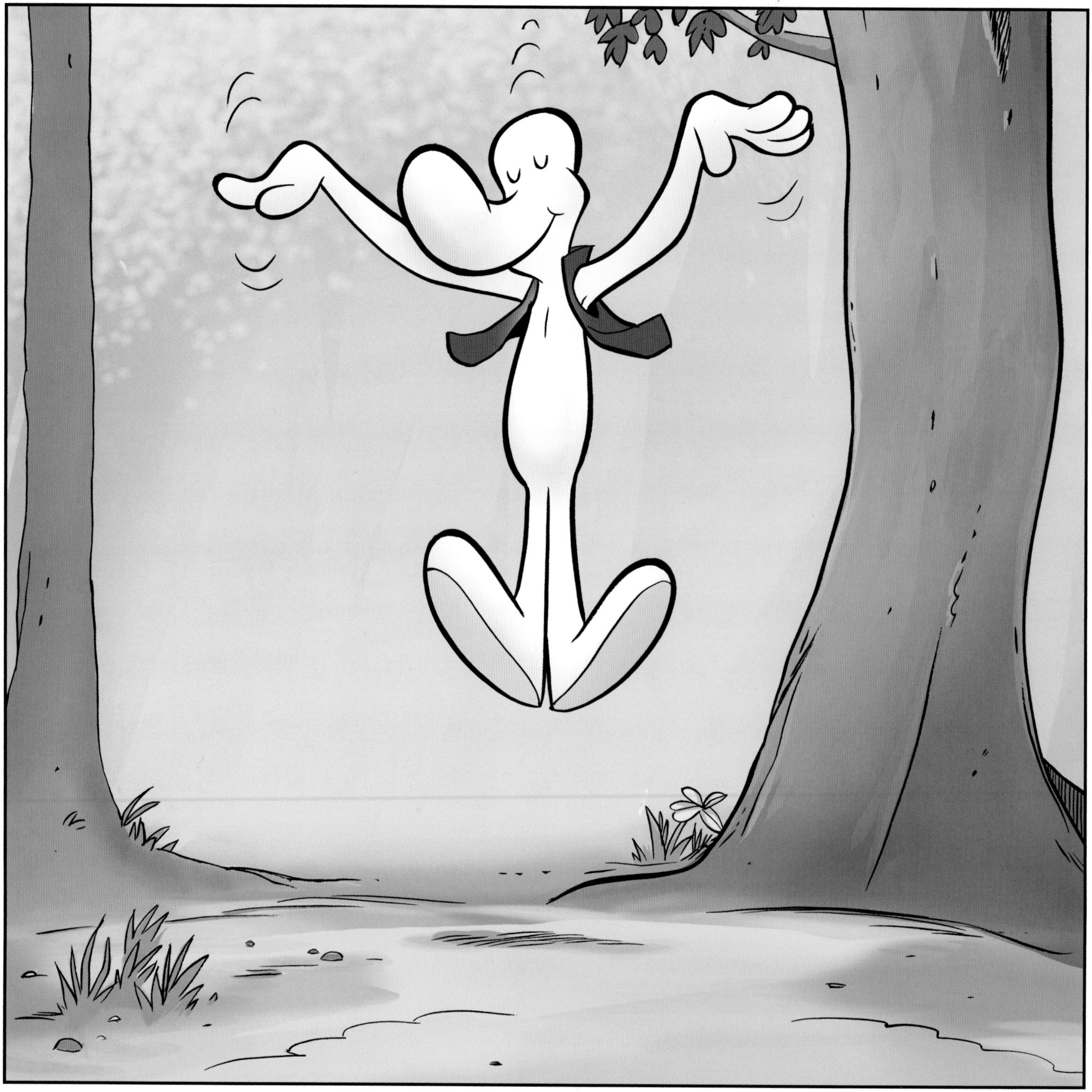

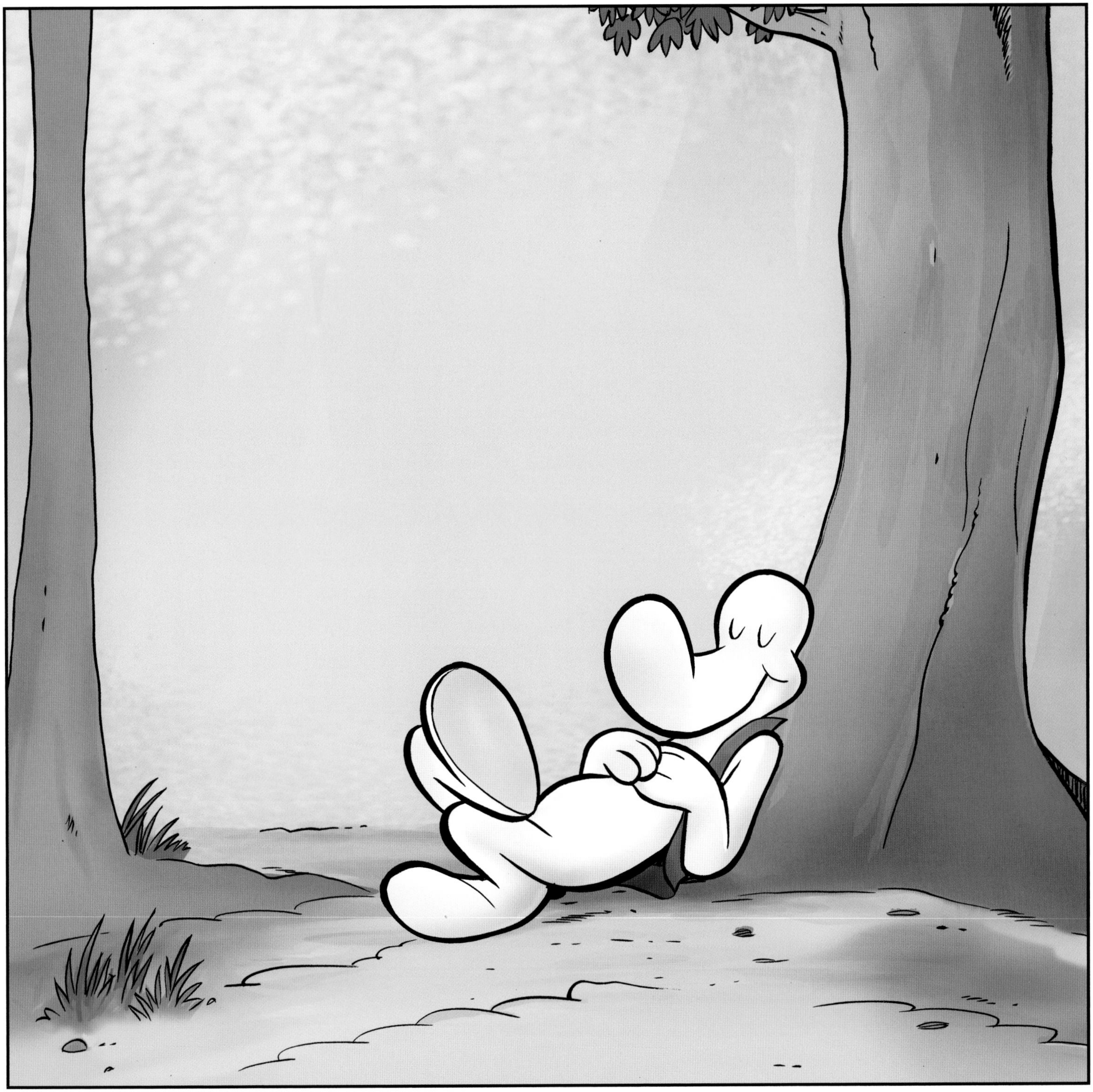

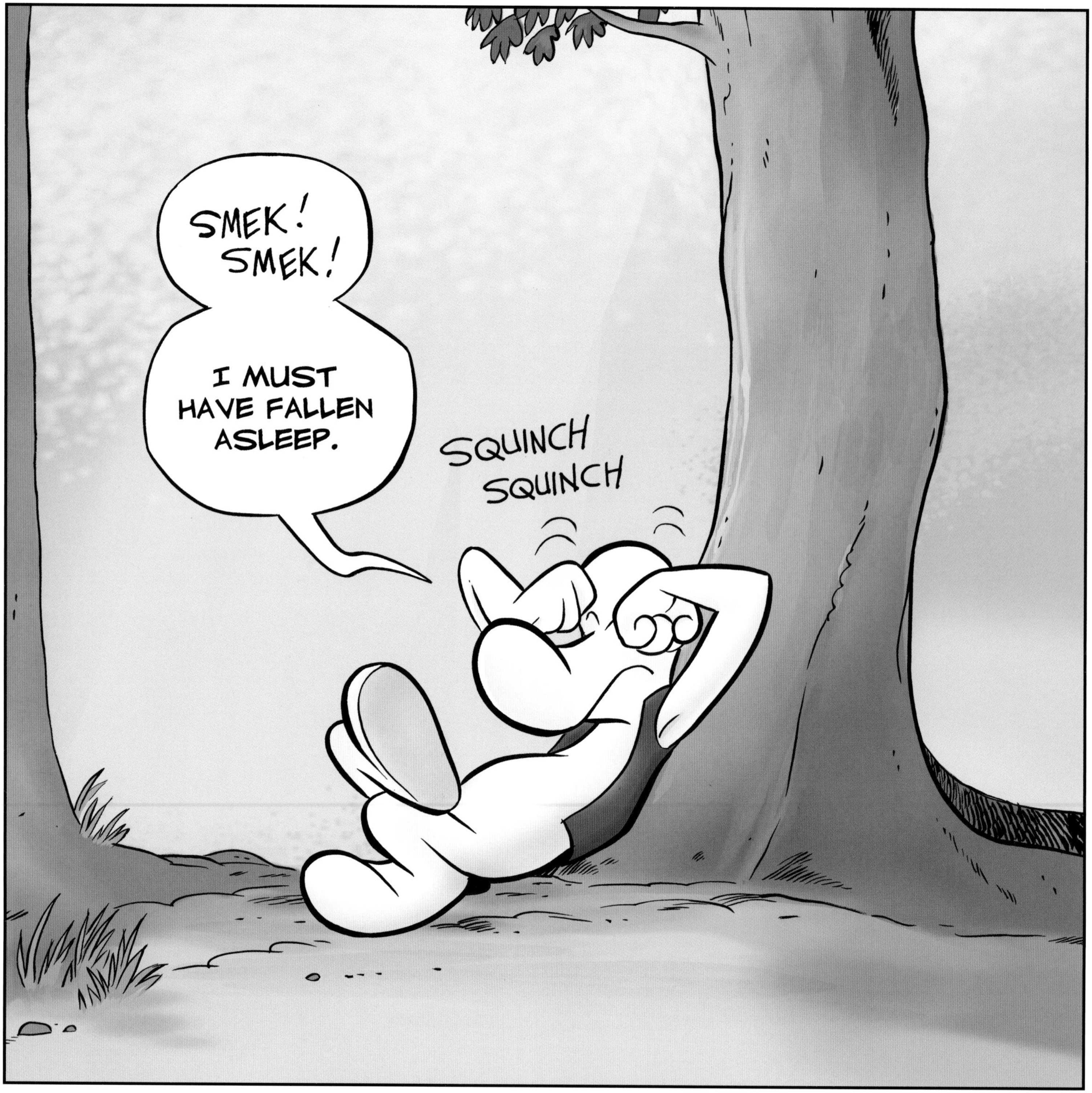
SMEK! SMEK!
I MUST HAVE FALLEN ASLEEP.
SQUINCH SQUINCH

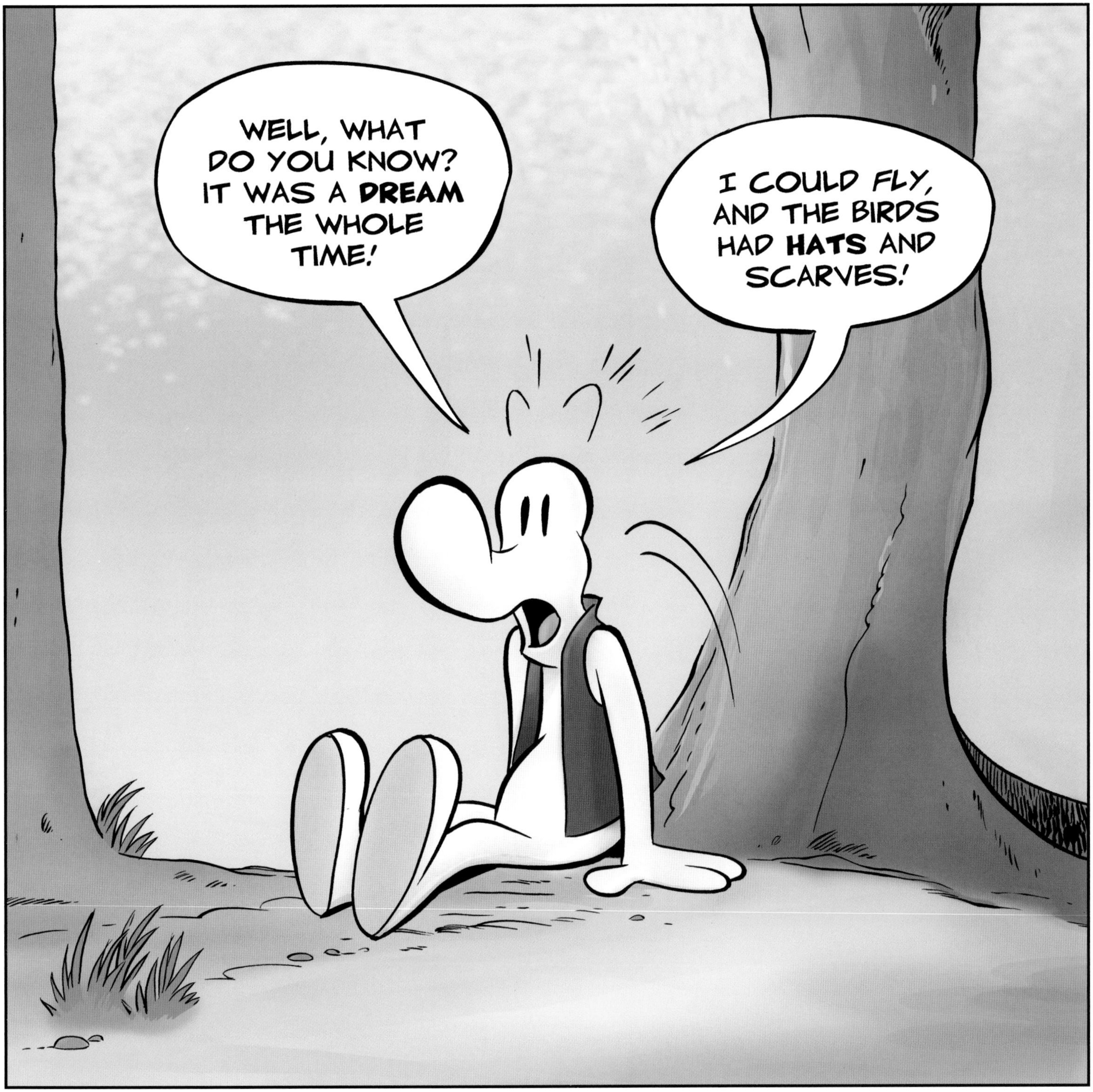
WELL, WHAT DO YOU KNOW? IT WAS A **DREAM** THE WHOLE TIME!
I COULD *FLY*, AND THE BIRDS HAD **HATS** AND SCARVES!

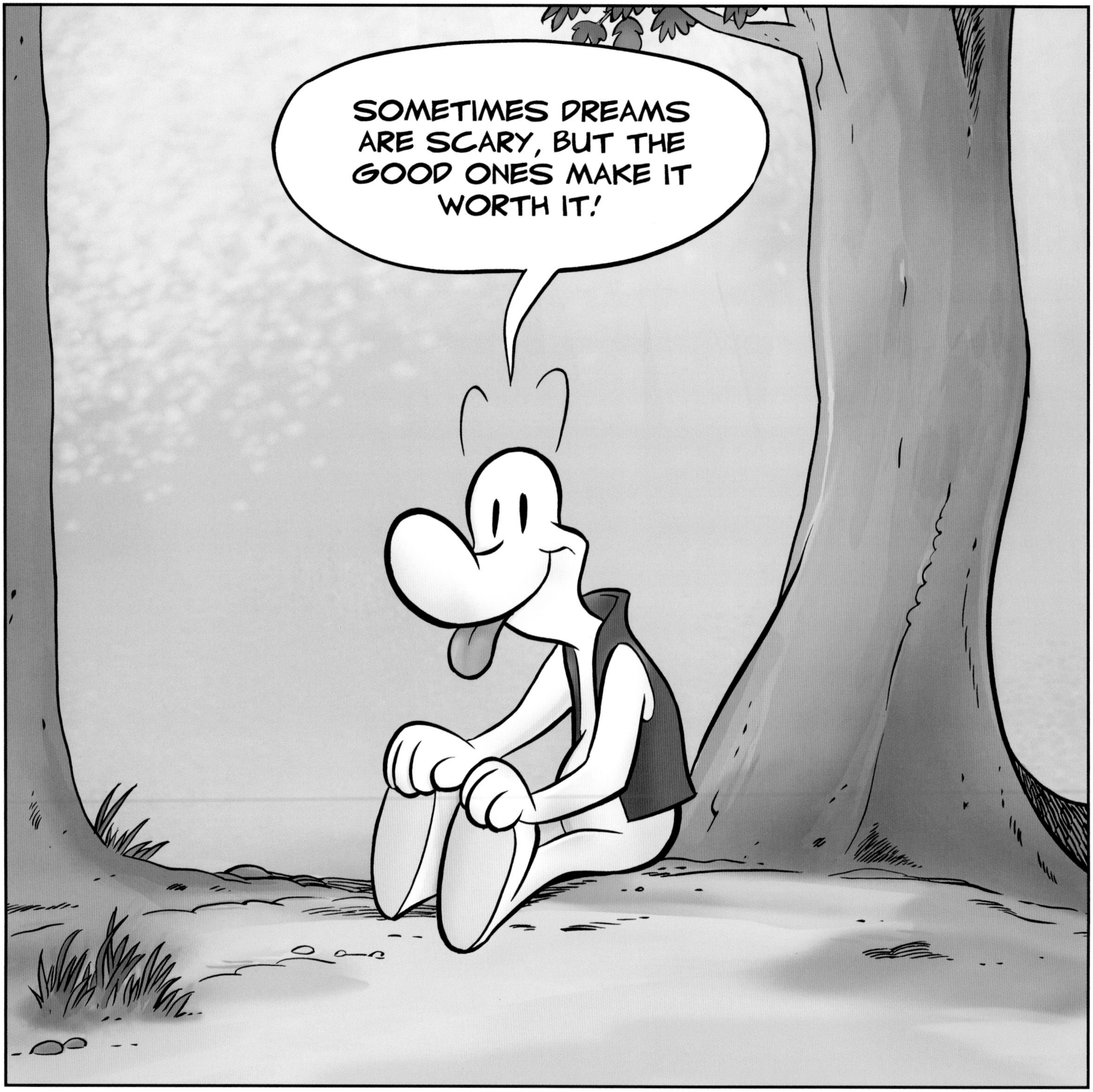
SOMETIMES DREAMS ARE SCARY, BUT THE GOOD ONES MAKE IT WORTH IT!

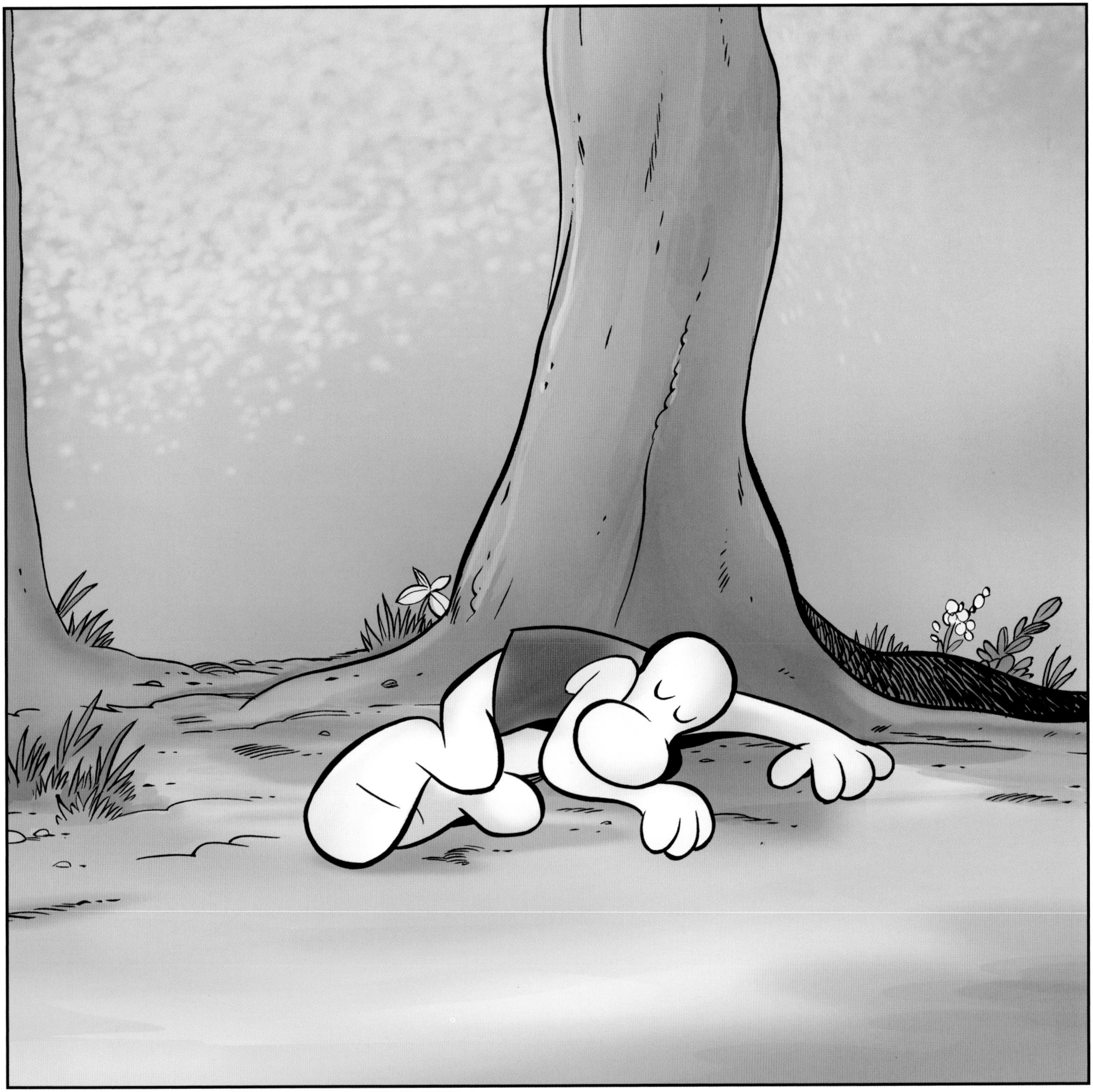

JEFF SMITH is the *New York Times* bestselling author of the award-winning BONE series, which is published in over 30 countries and is among *Time* magazine's Ten Best Graphic Novels of All Time. BONE was a pioneer in comics publishing for kids when it launched Scholastic's graphic novel imprint, Graphix, in 2005.

Smith's other award-winning and acclaimed comics include *SHAZAM! The Monster Society of Evil*, RASL, *Little Mouse Gets Ready!*, *Rose*, and *Tall Tales*. Smith splits his time between Columbus, Ohio, and Key West, Florida, with his wife and business partner, Vijaya Iyer. He's busy working on his current project, *TUKI: 2 Million BCE*.

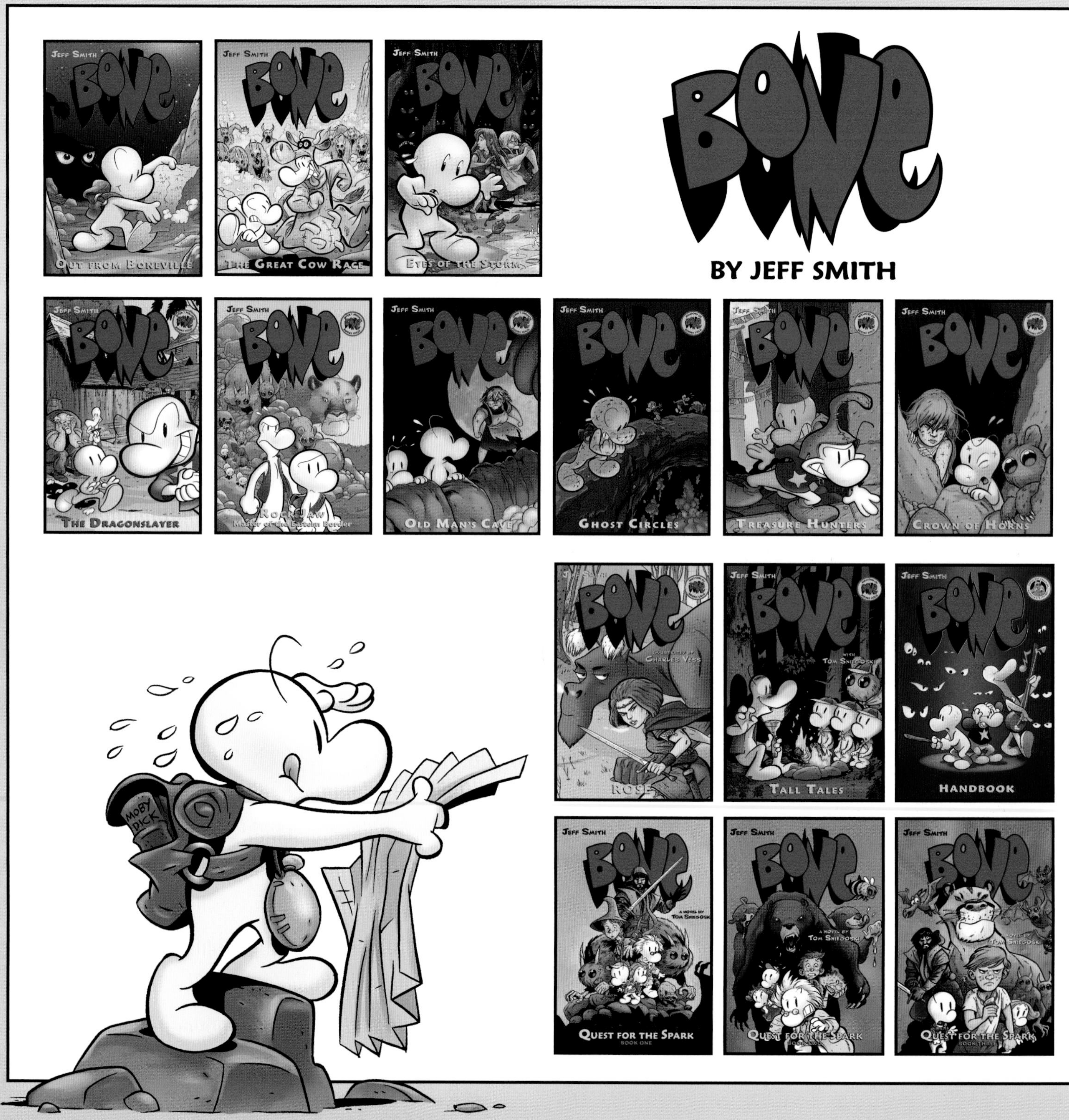
BONE
BY JEFF SMITH
JEFF SMITH BONE OUT FROM BONEVILLE
JEFF SMITH BONE THE GREAT COW RACE
JEFF SMITH BONE EYES OF THE STORM
JEFF SMITH BONE THE DRAGONSLAYER
JEFF SMITH BONE ROCK JAW Master of the Eastern Border
JEFF SMITH BONE OLD MAN'S CAVE
JEFF SMITH BONE GHOST CIRCLES
JEFF SMITH BONE TREASURE HUNTERS
JEFF SMITH BONE CROWN OF HORNS
BONE illustrated by CHARLES VESS ROSE
JEFF SMITH BONE with TOM SNIEGOSKI TALL TALES
JEFF SMITH BONE HANDBOOK
JEFF SMITH BONE a novel by TOM SNIEGOSKI QUEST FOR THE SPARK BOOK ONE
JEFF SMITH BONE a novel by TOM SNIEGOSKI QUEST FOR THE SPARK BOOK TWO
JEFF SMITH BONE a novel by TOM SNIEGOSKI QUEST FOR THE SPARK BOOK THREE
MOBY DICK